Whispering Loud and Clear

Life, Love, Laughter and The Spirit Among Us

∞

Trust!

Stuart Revercomb

www.whisper1.com

Copyright © 2002 by Stuart Revercomb

Whispering Loud and Clear
by Stuart Revercomb

Printed in the United States of America

Library of Congress Control Number: 2002112618
ISBN 1-591603-11-0

All rights reserved. No part of this publication may be repro-
duced or transmitted in any form or by any means without
written permission of the publisher.

Xulon Press
11350 Random Hills Road
Suite 800
Fairfax, VA 22030
(703) 279-6511
XulonPress.com

To order additional copies, call 1-866-909-BOOK (2665).

For The Reverend William R. Klein

*"All moments are key moments
and life itself is grace."*

- Frederick Buechner

Contents

1	The Most Amazing Incredible Thing	11
2	Dances With Angels	15
3	Image Is Everything?	21
4	Any Given Moment	25
5	The Unseen Here and Now	31
6	Fishing at Al's	35
7	Peace From The Weather Channel	39
8	The Greatest Sport in the World	43
9	The Better Side of Golf	49
10	The Goodness of Man	55
11	An Unpaved Paradise	59
12	The Judge	63
13	It's Black and White	67
14	It's a Willys Truck	71
15	Just a Coincidence	75
16	Thanks for the Memories	81
17	Jerry Rice Figures It Out	85
18	Goodbye Sweet Abbey	89
19	Big George's Day of Grace	93

Whispering Loud and Clear

20	Fish of Grace: Jim's Fish	99
21	Fish of Grace: Our Fish	103
22	Fish of Grace: Broaddy's Fish	107
23	Big Bangs and Buckyballs	113
24	Fishing for Eternity	117
25	Attitude is Everything	123
26	"The Perfect Flu"	127
27	Trust	131
28	Nothing to Fear But Fear Itself?	137
29	Hymn Singing 101	143
30	Going Up?	147
31	Out of the Mouths of Babes	151
32	Big Winning Hearts	155
33	Two Different Lives	159
34	What Do You Expect?	163
35	True Patriotism	167
36	All in Time	171
37	How "Successful" Are You?	177
38	Skating on Grace	181
39	The Best and Worst of Baseball	185
40	The Greatest Stories Are the Untold Stories	191

1

The Most Amazing Incredible Thing

Dads are great. Just when you think they've offered you about all the wisdom left in their well, they lower the old bucket one more time and bring up a refreshing bit of perspective that you never considered. Recently Pop splashed me with a good bit of insight, but as is often the case these days, I had to go digging for it.

Once Dads reach the venerable age of 65, they no longer offer the words that we so often refused to hear in our youth. Somewhere along the line they realize the only time we're apt to pay attention at all, is when we've posed a question ourselves. Accordingly, they ease into their late life "sage stage" —a point at which, garnering the wisdom of their years, they are able to sit back and await the moment of our approach with the false indifference of an experienced matador.

"Pop, you've grown up and lived in a rather interesting time. You've witnessed the results of the industrial and technological revolutions as well as the birth of the 'information age.' You've beheld the advent of the telephone, radio, television, nuclear fusion, all manner of medical miracles unthinkable 50 years ago, space travel, the wonder of super computers, the rise and fall of various world powers and the

Whispering Loud and Clear

birth of the Internet. What an absolutely amazing period of human progress . . . Dad, what is the most amazing, incredible thing that has occurred in your lifetime?"

Pop pondered a moment, but no longer than about five seconds (sages don't need much time to think about such things) and replied clearly and simply,

"Kroger."

I hesitated a moment and then eyebrows raised, asked incredulously, "Kroger?"

"Yes," he replied. "Kroger."

I really didn't get it. "Uh . . . , Kroger? Dad . . . , Why did you say Kroger?"

"Because, you just asked me what is the most amazing thing I have witnessed, so I said Kroger."

This is, of course, a form of bantering all fathers use with their sons, not so much wishing to appear "ignorant like a fox" as to keep them off balance at all times. Pretending to be distracted becomes a technique by which to level the playing field with sons who don't always listen. It also helps to focus our attention by making us ask the question a second time.

"Yes, I know that Dad, but WHY Kroger? I mean why in the world is Kroger the most amazing occurrence in your lifetime?"

"What do you suppose Genghis Khan, Alexander the Great and Henry VIII had for dinner most nights?"

"I'm sure I don't know Pop."

"Well I can tell you one thing. It wasn't what you and I eat. The Kings of the past would have traded the better part of their kingdoms for one Kroger down the street, and so would your Grandmother if she had had one to trade. When I was young, we ate whatever was in-season and sometimes whatever was available. We didn't have freezers, and refrigerators didn't come on the scene in any ordinary sense until the 1940's. Like everyone else we had an "ice box," and we

The Most Amazing Incredible Thing

mostly used it to keep dairy products cool. On summer afternoons your Grandmother would send a couple of us down to the corner store and we pretty much brought home what everyone else brought home. If they had pork and fresh corn that day, that's what we had. There was never a whole lot of choice in the matter. And it's not like we lived out on a farm or anything—this was in the middle of a relatively large city of over 60,000 at the time. I do not recall eating a fresh vegetable in winter until some time in the mid sixties."

"Think about it. You can walk into any large supermarket and procure all manner of the most extraordinary and fresh cuisine from literally every corner of the globe. King Crab from the Pacific, bananas from South America—dates, figs and spices from the Mideast and the Orient. Fish that were swimming two days ago in the North Atlantic are available to ranchers in Texas and lettuce that is picked in California on a Tuesday is presented to you crisp and fresh on Thursday. The variety of individual products alone is astounding. Did you say mustard? Which of the 127 kinds would you like?

Processing facilities and techniques used to provide the world's population with everything from bread and wine to meat and cheese are more recent than you might realize, and the innovations and inventions relative to transportation that make it all possible are so far beyond my boyhood imagination that I can hardly put words to it. To me the most unthinkable and amazing thing that has had the biggest impact on both the human race and me as an individual, is the availability of food as we know it. In a word..."

"Kroger," I said.

"You got it—Kroger," he said.

"I had no idea."

"I know, that's why I told you."

I thought about what he had said a moment more. "What do you think will be the most amazing thing to occur in your

Whispering Loud and Clear

Grandchildren's lifetime?"

"I don't know," he paused briefly. "Perhaps it will be a whole wide world of 'Krogers,' in every country—one on every corner, for everyone. They wouldn't have to carry everything, but enough for people to eat, such that little children didn't starve." He pursed his lips and then grimacing slightly looked at the ground and then at me. "Seems unlikely doesn't it?"

"No more than today's grocery stores would to two wide eyed boys walking home with a bag of pork and corn," I replied.

"No, I don't suppose so," he said with a smile.

Somehow it seemed like he had been waiting to say that.

Thanks, Pop. I hope you're right.

2

Dances With Angels

We all do stupid things.
Some more stupid than others.

My latest really stupid thing began as a really bright thing . . . at least it seemed that way at the time. I found myself at the top of a ladder perched about thirty feet above the ground. In my left hand was a heavy duty extension cord—in my right, a bale of colored Christmas lights. I had just completed wrapping the end of the extension cord around the top of the down spout on the corner of my house when it hit me. I was going to die doing this one day.

My wife had purchased these lights last year as an addition to the big colored bulbs we always hang on the portico above the front door of our house. Now here I was getting ready to hang them again. Somewhere, the voice of reason or angels or something whispered, "If you do something twice, it becomes tradition . . . and you know how you are about tradition. In a few years you're going to find yourself thinking that you HAVE to hang the lights . . . and that you're not TOO OLD to hang the lights . . . even though you REALLY ARE TOO OLD to hang the lights, and you're going to climb up here and the next thing you know you'll be headed for the ground, and you will either die or spend so long in traction that you wish you had."

Whispering Loud and Clear

Somehow I knew the voice was right. I promptly disconnected the extension cord from the unstrung bale and dropped it to the ground. I carefully descended the steep ladder, thankful beyond measure that I wouldn't have to venture back up in a few weeks to take them down. But when I stood out in front of the house with just the other lights hung, things looked rather barren. "What will the children think?" I questioned. I knew the answer. They were going to plead endlessly that I put the lights back up there—unless I could put something else up in their place. I pondered a moment. "Hmm . . . Yes! That was it! And easy too!"

We have an Angel banner we hang every year from our flag pole, but this year I had hesitated to replace the stars and bars for obvious reasons. I could use the ladder to safely get on top of the portico, and then stand up to easily hang the banner beneath the top eve of the house. I had an old shop light that would clamp on to the top of the gutter for illumination. It would be perfect.

Twenty minutes later the plan was executed. I surveyed it a moment before showing the wife, who seemed to like it as much as I did. It really did look pretty good, and besides, I remarked, "there are some nice theological implications—the Angel heralding the good news up above with all the tacky lights that represent the commercialism of the season below . . . "

"Hadn't thought about that," she replied. "It does look nice, though."

"Perfect," I thought as I placed the ladder alongside the house to be used again in a couple of weeks.

Only it wasn't quite perfect. A couple of hours later I noticed that a light breeze had flipped the Angel up on the roof. Her two feet that protruded slightly below the banner had become caught in the gutter. I hauled out the heavy ladder again and climbed back atop the portico. After contemplating several solutions I decided to weight the Angel's feet

Dances With Angels

with two, quarter pound lead fishing weights attached with safety pins. They would easily hold her down in the light breeze. But as I headed back down, I remember thinking that I would have to keep an eye on the weather forecast lest a strong wind come along and blow the Angel from her perch on high.

The best laid plans . . .

I did watch the weather forecast.

For about two days.

And the third day it hit—a Roanoke version of a Hatteras Noreaster. Except it wasn't exactly day—it was night . . . About 3:57 A.M. to be exact. I came out of bed as though shot from a cannon, which it seemed was exactly what someone was using to assault the front of our house.

"BAM! BAM! BAM! . . . KA-BAM! BAM!! BAM, BAM, BAM, BAM, BAM, BAM, BAM!!!

Silence.

KER-WHACK!!! BAM! BAM! BAM! . . . BAM!!! The Angels lead tipped feet were dancing a jig upon the front of our house, and she wasn't stepping lightly.

It was twenty-two degrees outside. I was standing in our darkened hallway in my boxer shorts. The wind was howling, providing a wind chill of God only knows what. Could I leave her up there until morning? No way, it might be waking the neighbors up. From the sound inside our house it was waking people up downtown. Besides, there might not be any bricks left by morning. Somehow the wife and children were still sleeping. I threw on some jeans and a sweatshirt and dashed down the stairs.

The words, "you are such an idiot," began playing in my head to the tune of "Rudolph the Red Nose Reindeer."

Halfway down the steps, I envisioned one of the Angel's feet whipping in the wind and catching me on the side of the head as I attempted to take it down. The "Darwin Awards" came to mind—awards given out every year to people who

17

Whispering Loud and Clear

manage to kill themselves in some exceedingly stupid way and who, it is implied, do us all a favor by not passing their genes along with the rest of the human race.

At the moment I was looking like a pretty good candidate.

I made my way out, barely managing to hold the door as the wind worked to wrench it from my hands. I struggled to close it and then headed down the steps. As soon as I came out from beneath the portico I looked up. Our Angel appeared to be holding on to the gutter for dear life—her feet performing an amazing staccato dance upon the bricks behind her. Fred Astaire would have been proud. No. Fred Astaire would have been in awe.

I zipped around the side of the house and retrieved the forty-foot aluminum extension ladder. It's amazing how quiet you can be with one of those things when your dignity is on the line. But the lanyards used to raise the upper section began to ping loudly against the rungs in the wind as I raised it against the house. I just knew my neighbor was going to show up with a camera any minute.

I was going to have to wrestle him for the film.

Securing the ladder, I made my way up to the top edge of the portico. It was at this moment that I realized that I actually was in some peril. The wind was easily gusting over thirty-five miles per hour and those lead weights appeared to be traveling even faster as they reached the end of the flag's reach and then randomly whipped about in every direction. BAM, BAM, BAM, BAM . . . KA-WHACK!!

"Better wait for a break in the wind," I thought.

Finally it came, and with all the skill of a mountain climber whose life depends on his next move, I scrambled up the portico roof and snatched the bar from which the Angel hung. She hugged me tightly in relief as the wind wrapped the material around the length of my body. We scrambled down the rooftop and then on to the ladder. It was quite the tango. She didn't let up until we had reached the

Dances With Angels

ground. I was breathing very heavily. She, on the other hand, was remarkably peaceful.

"I am so sorry," I said.

"That's O.K.—thanks for coming to get me," she replied.

Inside the house everything seemed strangely silent—no wind—no horrific banging—no more hollow metal beating of the lanyards against the ladder rungs. I gently folded the Angel on the dining room table and returned to my bed. It was 4:15 A.M.. The whole rescue had taken less than twenty minutes. My mind stopped racing about an hour later . . . just after I had devised a way to tie the Angel's feet off with fishing line.

Good traditions get easier every year.

3

Image Is Everything?

Image is NOT everything and clothes do not make the man.

But don't tell my son George that. I'm not sure where he got it, but at age six George actually cares about what he wears. Things must be the proper color. Patterns must "go together." Certain days require certain attire. In short, things must match. They must be "right.".

O.K. I lied. I actually do know where he got it. It was from his mom, because it certainly wasn't from me. I am soon to be 39, and one thing I have NEVER been accused of is being a "slave to fashion." I suspect I am still considered a rather lame dresser in the eyes of those who pay attention to styles and trends and whatnot, and likely in the eyes of those that don't as well.

I defer to the basics. Jeans or shorts with a tee or polo shirt on days when I have no meetings and feel the prospect of the impromptu one is pretty low. If the weather is going to be cool, I'll add a sweatshirt around my waist and head out the door. If I'm teaching, or a meeting is planned or possibly in the works, I'll "step out" in a pair of khakis and a "button-down" shirt.

I think people call them "Oxfords."

I'll also trade the Nikes in for a pair of Justin boots on

Whispering Loud and Clear

such days. The boots are deemed to be slightly dressier and are actually more comfortable than the tennis shoes. Their only drawback is that you can only run about two miles per hour in them. They also make for the occasional unexpected skate across parking lots and wet floors. I have windmilled my way into the hearts of complete strangers on more than one occasion. People feel sorry for young men who clearly cannot dunk a basketball, much less walk safely from one place to another.

I own five "Sunday go-to meeting" outfits and one blue blazer that I probably wear nine out of ten times that something more formal is required. But the suits do come in handy when I want to look like I belong in the business world or more at home with others at certain social gatherings. Given the option, however, they stay in the closet. I think there is a tux somewhere in the back, but I haven't seen it in a while.

I get exceptional tie mileage. Most of mine have been in and out of style at least three times. That's the great thing about ties—you can just keep wearing them, because sooner or later you're looking good again.

I remember wearing a pair of maroon bell bottom pants in the fifth grade so many times that a girl asked me if I owned any others. "Sure," I responded, "But why wear anything else when I like these best?" She looked at me kind of funny and walked off. It seemed like a strange question to me, but I took the hint and only wore them three out of five days the following week.

I have a picture of me and my girlfriend Kelly before some high school dance in the mid 70's. I have my arm around her and we are both smiling as if we are on our honeymoon. She is wearing a very attractive light peach chiffon number that could be worn by any woman, any age, anytime in the last 100 years and have been well received. I, on the other hand, am wearing PLAID RED AND WHITE PANTS

Image Is Everything?

with a matching RED TIE, WHITE COAT and RUFFLED SHIRT, the ruffles of which are TRIMMED IN RED. My hair compliments the suit nicely—someone has apparently been rubbing balloons on my head. I look like a cross between Danny Partridge and Julius Irving.

Every time I look at that picture, which is not often, I think, "My God, what was she doing with me?"

Later in life, if I had wanted to ruin her wedding plans, I could have done so by producing that picture for her husband-to-be. Reasonable doubt would have been more than well established. No one would have blamed him a bit if he had cut and run. Come to think of it, Kelly would likely pay big bucks for that thing even now. I'll hang on to it in case this writing thing ever goes south.

Which leads me back to son George.

He came into our room this morning all dressed for school. He had on a pair of dark tan khakis and a tee shirt that sported a soccer ball and a pair of cleats on the front. As is the norm with George, the colors of his selections actually matched, but the shirt was about two sizes too small and was coming apart at the seams. It was 38 degrees outside and raining. He didn't make it three paces into the room. "You need to change your shirt, George." He stood silently and listened to our list of reasons. This was followed by a heavy sigh and sulk from the room. I could remember my own such feelings as a child—"Why are THEY telling ME what to wear?"

So often, our parents reminded us that it's what's on the INSIDE that counts, but when it came to personal appearance we had better be up to social expectations. It was a lesson that was confusing from the start and further complicated by reality. Down the road in life we all meet people who are not what their cover advertises them to be. Good-looking well mannered individuals turn out to be crooks and cheats and the real slobs of life. While folks who

Whispering Loud and Clear

we initially wouldn't trust with a congenial greeting become lifelong friends. At the same time, the opposite is true. There are plenty of people who genuinely represent themselves— flying their true colors regardless of their nature.

How is one to know?

One isn't. The trick is simply to avoid forming too many preconceptions. The proper balance of trust, intuition and prudent inquiry can go a long way. Unless, of course, the guy is wearing red and white plaid pants . . . in which case run like hell and don't look back.

Someone could have a camera.

4

Any Given Moment

I am 28. We are in the Bahamas. My brother Jim and I, and four other ne'er do wells, have "bare boated" a 38-foot sailboat from Fort Lauderdale to Grand Bahama Island and we are preparing to go snorkeling over an uncharted reef. It is a bright and beautiful island kind of day—no clouds, no phones, no worries . . . nobody for about 200 miles.

    We have anchored about 150 yards off the reef as the draft of the boat is about six feet and our charts do not seem to agree with the depth provided by our sonar. My friend Bob and I are the first into the water. We probably should take the dinghy, but the open water swim is inviting. We make good progress through the light chop and in a few minutes are just above the main part of the reef looking back at the yacht—its 60 foot mast sways gently above the lanyards and royal blue "Bimini Top." Travel magazine photographers must search hard for just such a day—a boat—a moment.

    "Ouch," I muffle past the rubber stopper in my mouth. Sinking in the trough of a wave I have banged my knee on part of the reef. Looking through my mask underwater I examine the skin and in the still and quiet my leg somehow does not seem to be my own. Decent cut, but not bad. Certainly no stitches required. I give it a rub and move on, fol-

lowing Bob who has gone deeper looking for a rock lobster to
skewer for lunch. Several minutes pass as we repeatedly rise
and return to the new discoveries that seem to come every few
moments on such a reef.

Instantly, he is there—a large Atlantic Barracuda. Not
like the one to two foot variety we are accustom to, but a
four-foot "mother" as we would later describe him. I tap
Bob on the shoulder to draw his attention and he puts up his
hand without turning his head as he thinks he's on the verge
of corralling a lobster. I tap him again and he repeats the
"Hold On" signal. I check for the Barracuda who is now
much closer. I tap Bob slower and with the firmness of
someone who means it. Bob turns his head looking somewhat annoyed and I point him off to my right where the
Barracuda has been hovering.

Bob's eyes get VERY, VERY BIG.

"Strange," I think to myself, the Barracuda is by far the
biggest I've ever seen and those are some mean looking
teeth, but Bob is probably the most fearless among us. I look
back to where I'm pointing him and my heart stops in mid-
beat. The Barracuda is no longer in sight. In its place is a
nine-foot Shark who is clearly as interested in us as we are
now in him.

Up to that point in my life I had never really thought
about swimming with a very large shark. I guess the odds
seemed so remote—and then somehow, we were thinking
about a trip, and then talking about it, and then making
plans, and then on a train, and on a plane . . . and now somehow in the water. It all seems so surreal. I just didn't plan on
it . . . but "it" apparently has planned on me. For a moment
more I think, "yes, this is a dream." But the blood seeping
from my knee indicates otherwise.

He circles us slowly. Bob and I both immediately give a
response apparently stored within the genes of all Homo
Sapiens. Independent of each other, we instantly spread our

arms and legs out in a kind of floating crouch position attempting to look as large as possible. This seems to work to some degree as the shark, as far as I can tell, is not yet ready to eat us. But we have one other fairly significant problem. We can not breathe. I began to slowly flipper my way to the surface. Bob follows. We are side by side now, slowly turning in unison, as the shark steadily circles, rising with us as we go. Our snorkels finally break the surface and we clear them with a burst of air. We watch the shark for a moment more and then Bob, his eyes still wide and intense, gives the universal thumbs up for communication. We lift our heads above the water and Bob frantically rips out his snorkel and yells, voice cracking, "Wha . . . Wha . . . Whatever you do . . . da, da don—DON'T PANIC !!" He jams the snorkel back between his lips and is back beneath the water before I can respond.

"Well, that's some helpful advice," I think to myself. Truthfully, if I had attempted any words at that moment they would have been much the same. I immediately slip back beneath the surface and scan the water intently.

The shark is still there, but this time a little closer. He comes in slowly from his orbit to within about ten feet and then returns to what I hesitate to describe as a "safer" distance of perhaps twenty-five. His coal black eyes are prehistoric and cold and he moves so effortlessly through the warm clear water that there is little doubt about who owns the moment. He is calculating and precise and every sweep of his taut grey body, seems choreographed by something nameless and dark. It is the poetry of nature to be sure, but the threat is real and present and potentially deadly.

Yet, somehow I begin to feel an unspeakable calm about me that seems totally beyond my ability to create it. I am beginning to sense something on a level I never have before. It is a gentle whisper amidst the adrenaline charged intensity of the moment—life is precious and fragile and real and something . . . something more . . .

Whispering Loud and Clear

It is ten years later. I am in my car and life couldn't be greater. We are headed to the beach. My wife is in the back with the children. They are singing to a "sing-along" tape and laughing. We have brought a baby sitter along for the trip—Juanetta is in the passenger seat up front with me. We are on a wide open and well-maintained stretch of North Carolina highway. There are few cars on the road and oddly enough I have just thought to myself how wonderfully peaceful and calm the moment seems to be.

We are approaching a car on the side of the road. A man has run out of gas. He has just come around the back of the vehicle with a gas can, having exited a white pickup truck that is parked in front of him. Juanetta begins to speak, "Look, he's run out of . . . Watch . . . !" She can say no more. The truck parked in front does not see us and has cut his wheel hard to cross over through the median. He is blocking both lanes about twelve feet in front of us. We are traveling at seventy miles per hour. There is no time to react. I do not know what is to the left of us, but I do know we are going there. My hands seem to turn the wheel before I can even think, and we are off the road and sliding and bouncing across the V shaped median heading for oncoming traffic. My best guess is that we have missed the pickup by 3 or 4 inches. As we begin to cross the grass in the intensity of the moment, I hear four words—"We can do this," they say. They repeat themselves.

I feel remarkably calm and somehow the grass and mud beneath our wheels feel familiar. Perhaps I am remembering the days of my youth on our farm driving faster than I should through the fields and pastures. I lobby myself heavily to resist the temptation of the brakes. Gaging the remaining distance to the oncoming traffic, I slowly begin to coax the wheel back toward the middle of the median. We slide—we straighten—we slide—we straighten again and then begin to descend back toward the bottom of the "V." Bam! We cross

Any Given Moment

a drainage grate and begin to decelerate, sixty . . . forty-five
. . . thirty. I look in my rear view mirror and see that traffic
on both sides of the highway has stopped. The car that has
nearly taken our lives has just finished crossing the median
and is racing north behind us—the driver not wanting to face
our wrath or his own culpability. I ease the van back up the
median while we still have momentum. We come out onto
the black top and coast along in the right-hand lane. The sing
along tape continues—"Oh, How I Love Jesus—Oh How I
Love Jesus—Because He First Loved Me . . . "

One of the children begins singing. Our two-month-
old is still asleep. The morning is seemingly no different
than before.

Except we are different—changed in a moment of overwhelming terror that has confronted us when we least
expected it. But it has been met with an equally unexpected
and life affirming presence that speaks in such moments
abiding and reassuring and mysterious. Win, lose or draw it
is somehow extravagantly and unconditionally for us.

As time goes by, the things of this world will have me
thinking less and less of the Peace I found in the water that
day or vectoring off that highway in half the apparent distance needed to miss that car. I will not hear the words of
comfort and assurance as clearly . . . they will likely continue
to fade into the predictable and rational fabric of things. But
not completely, for I know in my heart that the Spirit, while
mostly whispering quietly in the everyday moments of our
lives, can and does move boldly among us as well—alive and
present and real when we need him the most.

And thanks be to God for that.

5

The Unseen Here and Now

I am on vacation. We are in Florida, and NOTHING is happening.
Which is EXACTLY what we want.
The kids are behaving. The weather is perfect, and I am lying on my stomach on a turquoise pool float. I am not in the pool but next to it. The float has been in the sun a while and is now very warm. It is taking the light chill of the water from my body.
I am VERY comfortable.
My eyelids seem to involuntarily open and close. The palm trees are gently floating in the breeze and the sky is that technicolor blue you mostly only see in 1940's John Wayne movies. Life at the moment is quite good. In fact, it's about as close to perfect as I tend to find it. I am thinking of nothing significant, and as far as I can tell, nothing significant is presently thinking of me.
Something catches my attention on the slate in front of me. It is a colony of ants.
The pool is on my right. There is a two-foot wide "border garden" on my left and grass beyond. The ants are working the slate surface in between—juking and jiving and cutting and turning in all directions and in no direction at once. Somehow, amidst their seemingly random dance, they

are affecting an end result that is generally a straight line from the edge of the raised concrete pool perimeter to the mulch of the border garden. Their bustling activity stirs my thoughts.

I am reminded that the rest of the world is not on vacation. I can hear the sound of construction equipment a couple of blocks away and the faint whisper of passing cars on the busy beach road around the corner. Big things are happening in faraway places—power and money are changing hands. Careers are being made and lost. The earth presses on in its persistent journey around the sun and somewhere in the distant cosmos planetary bodies must collide, but just like me, these ants know nothing of it. And all of humanity and creation, save me, knows nothing of them.

What are they thinking, I wonder?

I regard them a moment more and realize that every so often a single ant emerges from the mulch on the left, clutching some sort of prize before him. Mostly, they appear to be small articles of plant debris, but every now and then, one emerges with what appears to be part of another bug. One passes by with the wing of something that is several times bigger than he is. I am reminded that "pound for pound" ants are the strongest living thing on the planet. Several more pass by and then one emerges from the mulch with what appears to be a beetle's abdomen.

"Now there's a nice find," I think. "The queen will be singing his praises tonight."

But his luck is short-lived. A larger ant coming from the other direction attempts to wrestle his prize away. They grapple several seconds and it appears briefly that the smaller, original owner might come out victorious, but the attacker is simply too big. He wrenches the prize free and turns back—going with the flow of ants towards the border of the pool that apparently leads to home.

"That is so unjust," I think. "Nature can be so cruel. No

The Unseen Here and Now

telling how long that little guy worked for that thing."

For a moment, my mind wanders to debate the reality of free-will and chance and the very real randomness with which things so often seem to happen. My thoughts skip to several sad events that have recently played themselves out in the news. My sense of human justice quickly has me questioning the necessity of such a world.

"It's just not fair," I think.

And I'm right. According to my understanding of things, it's not.

I watch the big ant a moment longer, resisting the urge to dispense justice with my thumb. And apparently, in this thought, I am not alone. Slowly from around the other side of the pool ambles "Emma," my parents' overweight, under-intelligent, nine year old Golden Retriever. She has been chasing lizards along the side of the house. As she approaches, she lowers her head and increases the wag of her tail. The skin of her face droops long and she smiles in agreement with her disposition, which is 100 percent happy, 100 percent of the time.

She is approaching the column of ants. The little guy who has lost his prize is heading back and has almost made it to the edge of the mulch. The low-down cheat that has bullied his way to wealth is halfway to the other side. Emma moseys persistently forward—the big leather pads of her feet spreading out soft but firm under her lazy gait.

SKA-WHISH.

The rare moment of "random" justice comes with unexpected sweetness, and I smile up at Emma who has little notion of her role as judge, jury and executioner. She licks the top of my head and then sniffs the column of ants—the exhale of her nostrils blows several back into the mulch. She steps slowly over them in search of more lizards in the grass.

My son pops up from the bottom of the pool with a penny he has found.

Whispering Loud and Clear

"Look Dad—I didn't even know it was there!"

"I didn't either," I reply.

The world spins steadily on, full of mercy and mystery and magic—in the divine and infinite hour that is the unseen here and now.

6

Fishing at Al's

I took my little guys fishing the other day and we caught fish.
Big Rainbow Trout fish.
The kind you eat.
I once stalked such creatures as a gentlemen with reel and creel and fly. No longer. I have four children six and under. We fish with Zebcos. We fish with bobber and worm. We fish loud, and we fish fast. As far as George, Gussie and Jane are concerned, the more often you slap the water with that bobber, the more fish you're liable to catch. Only this time it wasn't working, and I was having a hard time convincing Jane, the youngest child of fishing age, that a quiet approach might better yield our quarry. She was having none of it.
"Cast Dad—I wanna cast."
Alas, the day was beautiful and the land was resplendent in its Spring apparel.
"Good day to get skunked if you have to . . . ," I thought. I laid back on the dock and soaked in the sun as every fish in the pond cowered on the bottom. The kids were having fun slinging those poor worms all over the place, so priority number one was being accomplished . . . .
We were at "The Virginia Country Mountain Center"

Whispering Loud and Clear

owned by my friend Al Hammond, who is certainly a column in and of himself. Al used to coach me in ninety pound City League Football. If you irritated him with sub-par play, he would paste your helmet with tobacco spit. It was a very effective deterrent to poor tackling. I don't guess coaches do that much these days, but maybe they should—I don't think Al ever lost a title.

The VCMC is what used to be his sheep farm, and I suppose I'll always think of it as such. But Al doesn't. He's on a mission. He wants folks to know that this part of Virginia is unlike any other place in the world. So he's taken his 340 acres that lie just north of Roanoke's Explore Park and created a place where others "can get an education" in everything outdoors—from hiking and canoeing to fly fishing and sporting clays. The center boast over ten miles of hiking and biking trails, one mile of river frontage, three stocked ponds, endless open fields and meadows and a view of the Roanoke Valley from the northeast that is as extraordinary as it is unique.

Before we began tormenting these fish, we had stopped by the conference center. Al and a friend were setting up for a youth program sponsored by the National Wild Turkey Federation. There was a Virginia State Fish and Wildlife Trailer parked outside that had hauled a large video simulator used in gun safety training. Al was in his usual good form.

"Well hey there Rever-burger! Welcome to Fort Apache! You can keep the fish if you catch them today . . . Need to thin 'em out for the summer . . . but you guys leave a few for me, will ya! "

The kids all yelled that they were going to catch every single fish on the property as they took off toward a new playground near the pavilion. "I'll try Al, but those are some pretty determined fishermen," I responded.

There was little danger of depleting the pond during our first forty minutes, but the casting frenzy finally calmed

Fishing at Al's

down and even Jane eventually decided to sit quietly in hopes of landing a "fishy." Lucky for us, these Trout were either brave or hungry or both. After about five minutes of relative quiet, son George's bobber "ploonked" beneath the surface and we all jumped up to see what he had.

The question should have been, "What had him?"

George's rod bent in a U shape and his eyes were wide with surprise and excitement. Whatever it was, it was indeed big. He had to spread his feet apart to steady himself on the dock.

I am convinced that the biggest challenge in all of sport-fishing is only experienced by those who fish with small children, and it comes with the maddening realization that Junior has a really, really big one on the line. The first instinct is to grab the rod and make sure that you get that "sure to be a state record" back to dry land. You then quickly remember that if you are any real Dad at all you will stay back, cheer him on and let him succeed or fail on his own— even if that does mean losing the only chance you'll ever have at a citation with the family name on it.

"It is not about the fish," you remind yourself.

Sounds easy. But when that eighteen inch, three pound, sparkling Rainbow Trout goes dancing across the water, it's not. In fact, it seems to be very much about the fish. But all you can do is coach as if the adrenaline charged ears of your son can actually hear you.

"Keep the tension on him George! Rod tip up high . . . Rod tip up!! Reel baby reel!!!"

My two daughters, ages five and three, were yelling and screaming and jumping and repeating after me:

"Keep tens on high, George! Rob-erts Up! Rob-erts Up! Reel the baby George—Reel the baby!"

Excitement was high. Confusion reigned and, lucky for us cheerleaders, so did George. He brought that fish in like a pro.

You already know the size.

37

Whispering Loud and Clear

Not long thereafter, Gussie and Jane hooked up with some respectable catches, and Dad once again managed to keep his hands together in prayer, in lieu of helping them reel. It's painful to watch a three-year-old slowly crank away at a beautiful Rainbow, but I suppose from the fish's perspective it's even worse. By the time Jane got hers to the dock, the fish had long since given up the struggle and was more than willing to be placed in the cooler.

We steamed them in butter that night on the grill.

Thanks, Al—It was a great education!

7

Peace From The Weather Channel

I have a confession to make. I LOVE the Weather Channel. That's right—it's a capital letter kind of love that maybe borders on an obsession. Omit football in the fall, and as far as I'm concerned there is little else worth watching. My wife thinks I'm nuts.

"How many low-pressure systems can you watch in one week?" she recently queried.

"Shhh! Weather Center is just starting . . . look at those isobars over Kansas. Sharon Resultan just said there were some "J hooks" on the local Doppler radar out of Wichita . . . may be a wild ride in the old alley tonight," I replied.

She rolled her eyes in frustration.

"We don't LIVE in Wichita," she responded. She hesitated a moment. "Oh goodness . . . look, I think she's pregnant again . . . " This remark was clearly an effort to rekindle our "Sharon Resultan debate." My normal viewing time coincides with Mrs. Resultan's nightly forecast, and it wasn't long ago the wife noted the correlation and jokingly asked if I was watching the weather or the weather person.

"For heavens sake," I replied, "she gives a good weather forecast!"

Whispering Loud and Clear

Not that I don't prefer her presentation to Jim Cantori's. "How many children has she had?", she asked.

"Three," I responded. "About the same ages as ours—except Jane. She didn't have one when we had Jane. If we're ever in Atlanta, we'll have to look them up."

She rolled her eyes even further this time.

"You HAVE been watching too much," she said in exasperation.

Maybe so. But if you're going to watch too much of anything, The Weather Channel's the place to be. A pregnant weather forecaster is about as close to controversial as you're going to get. It's a pretty stark contrast to the balance of fare offered in T.V. land these days.

Between the pornography so often served up by movie channels like HBO, and the never-ending stream of violence that is the staple of the networks and the so called "superstations," television offers a daily meal that is anything but healthy. You might say there are a lot of "fat grams" in the diet, and in this case they lead to a hardening of both the heart and the mind. Unfortunately, it is our children that most often sit down at the banquet table that is modern day cable and satellite television, and it is they who absorb the vast majority of its rancid offering.

In his book, "Abandoned in the Wasteland: Children, Television and the First Amendment," former FCC Chairman, Newton Minnow, states that, "by the time most Americans are eighteen years old, they have spent more time watching television than they have spent in school."

That's an AVERAGE of three-and-a-half hours a day 365 days a year.

Perhaps a more disturbing fact is that according to the American Psychological Association, "the typical American child will witness 8,000 murders and 100,000 acts of televised violence in his lifetime."

Eight-Thousand murders?

Peace From The Weather Channel

If you had taken the leading Psychologists of the 1940's and 50's and asked them what they thought the outcome would be of subjecting some poor child to such a fate, I suspect their answers would closely mirror the end product we so often see in our society today. I think the need for over 100,000 NEW prison cells a year would have been a safe projection. In reality, the average is 230,162 according to the Federal Bureau of Justice.

These are some pretty unsettling statistics, but they seem cold and stale as the mainstream of American culture continues to race by all around us, so colorful and seemingly vibrant. Even if we desperately wanted to do something, what could we?

Some guy named Paul wrote a letter about nineteen hundred years ago to some folks he knew in Rome, and in it he stated that he thought it would be a very good idea not to support things that tended to bring others down. Maybe he was on to something.

I don't suppose we need to throw all our T.V.'s out the window, but if those of us who cared about such things were to watch only that which lifted others up instead of causing them to stumble, we might start a trend towards better programming or maybe even a little less watching altogether.

Having a few more moments with our children might not be such a bad thing either.

So bring a little Peace to the world—watch the Weather Channel.

8

The Greatest Sport in the World

Move over Baseball. Take a back seat NFL. I've no time for your dribbling and whining NBA. Hockey's fun, but it hurts my ankles just to watch those guys skate. World Cup? Let 'em continue to kick that ball up and down the field, falling in mock agony every time they brush against each other. It makes no difference to me, because the greatest sport in the world is none of the above.

The greatest sport in the world is Crabbing.

In the unsophisticated 60's and 70's we crabbed in the timeless manner of our forefathers. We took the preferred bait of fish heads and chicken necks and tied them to a piece of string. We then lowered the skanky fare to the bottom and waited for Monsieur Crab to come along. Upon sensing something was grappling with our fifteen-cent fish head (or just having that "feeling") we would slowly and steadily pull the bait to the surface—all the while praying fervently that the crab would sense nothing of the ride to the boiling cauldron that had just begun. The major problem with this technique is that it was a two-man process that required a partner or "netter" to successfully swoop under the crab with a ring net attached to a pole.

Whispering Loud and Clear

It was here that the process often went south. Swooping crabs with a net is not a physical act one tends to practice while not on vacation, and when the majority of us arrived on our docks to perform this, the most artful move of the sport, we were not always in perfect form. Many a controversy broke out between "puller" and "netter" as a large crab dropped at the last second, back into the briny shallows.

"I CAN'T BELIEVE YOU MISSED HIM! HE WAS HUGE!!"

"WHAT?!!—IF YOU HADN'T BROUGHT HIM UP SO FAST, WE'D BE DUMPING HIM IN THE BUCKET RIGHT NOW!"

It wasn't an argument that was easily rested—it's not like we had instant replay or anything.

"YOU COULDN'T NET A GRAPEFRUIT FROM A TREE!"

"YOU COULDN'T BRING A BUBBLE TO THE SURFACE!"

The occasional argument aside, it was a ton of fun. There's something tremendously rewarding about bringing something unseen from the depths to the surface, and further still, into one's possession. When a fish is on the hook, you've accomplished most of the sport, but a crab is never in the books until he's boiling on the stove, which, thanks to some innovative crabbing technology, is a bit easier to accomplish these days.

It's called the "basket net." Or as my friend, Mark, has dubbed it: "The Skank-Master 2000."

The "Skank-Master" is a two-tiered basket that when lowered with fish head affixed in the middle, collapses to a flat surface on the bottom. When Monsieur Crab arrives on the scene you simply lift, and as long as you're not too lackadaisical, voila, you've got your crab. My three-year-old performed the operation successfully several times, shrieking with glee at her catch as it came out of the water and

The Greatest Sport in the World

then running for cover as soon as I took the line from her hands and began to swing the basket over the confines of the dock. She was perfectly willing to raise it out of the water, but she wasn't going to do battle with that thing on land.

This technique is a great deal more reliable than the method described earlier, but much of the original dare and suspense is lost. I guess you can call it progress, but when they're a little bit older you can bet my guys will be taught the early game of "pull and swoop." And when I think they're ready for the big time, I'll introduce them to the true pinnacle of the sport—Rock Crabbing.

There may be others who Rock Crab, but as far as I know, my friend Mark and I invented this aspect of the game in 1996 while poking around an oceanfront rock jetty at low tide. "Holy Cow! Look at the size of that Crab!" Mark yelled, as a huge specimen scurried from the rocks for open sea. He had been poking a broken shovel around the cracks and ledges just below the waterline. We looked at each other with eye brows raised in the manner of John Belushi.

"You don't suppose . . . "

We were off for the net and the bucket and back in no time.

Successful Rock Crabbing, we soon learned, takes the patience of dock crabbing, the timing of a cliff diver, the discipline of the martial arts and the courage of a lion tamer. Here's how it works:

Wearing NO SHOES, you take the pole end of your crab net and deftly poke and prod among the crevices as detailed in Marks first encounter. This is done in about two feet of water and must be timed in accordance with the onslaught of waves that crash every ten to fifteen seconds upon the rocks. To miss-calculate the wave is to put ones "podiatal digits" in great jeopardy, as the last thing you want to do is evoke the wrath of an Atlantic Blue Crab just before he and your bare toes disappear into the sandy backwash of a retreating wave.

These crabs don't scramble out running for cover.

Whispering Loud and Clear

Rather, having just been roused from their homes with what amounts to a broomstick, they emerge with their bright blue and orange pinchers raised high and open. The Atlantic Blue Crab is a great deal larger than his "creek" counterpart, and its claws can easily grip the largest of big toes. Sooner or later, an unforeseen wave will surprise the most adept rookie just as a crab emerges.

"AiiiiYYEEEEEEEEEE!!!"

A dripping wet, sunburned, "mature" 38 year old male, high stepping out of the surf, crab net high in hand, is indeed a sight to behold.

The object, of course, is not to flee from one's quarry, but rather to snare it, so as soon as the adrenaline level has come back and courage can again be mustered, reentry into the surf should be encouraged. It is generally at this point that the candidate feels he has been "beaten" by a creature whose brain stopped developing in the Mesozoic Period, so determination usually rises on its own.

With any luck, the next crab will be correctly flushed at the moment the water is losing its turbidity, and the crabber will be required to smoothly and quickly reverse the pole net in his hands much like Kwai Chang Kane used to do with those long sticks at the monastery. If he can keep his nerve, he has about three seconds in which to ascertain the crabs speed and direction and, allotting for the current of the retreating wave, swoop it up from the bottom of the sea.

If he fails to do so and fate has incorrectly positioned him in the path of the now ocean-going crab, he stands a good shot at being on the receiving end of a very painful pinch. But just knowing that crab is down there somewhere is often enough to induce panic. Many a Rock Crabber has brought his net up out of the swirling tempest of a receding wave with a smile on his face, and upon seeing it empty, proceeded to perform the aforementioned goose step while releasing an involuntary scream not unlike that heard from

The Greatest Sport in the World

movie actors while falling from a tremendous height.

It's great fun.

But why no shoes, you most surely ask?

Because, relative to dock crabbing without a "net basket," that's the thrill of it. To guarantee success, or to not risk oneself in pursuit of the goal, is to merely go through the motions of the game. You may wind up with more crabs in the short term, but pretty soon you won't be enjoying the endeavor, and shortly thereafter, you likely will have lost your zeal for the game completely. Meaning no crabs in the long term and no more fun along the way.

Perhaps if Marx and Lenin had Rock Crabbed, we'd have never suffered the scourge of Communism.

Risk and reward, challenge and chance . . . they seem to be a part of the heart of us, don't they.

The greatest game in all of sport?

Crabbing by a long shot.

9

The Better Side of Golf

I was born for this game. I love it. Problem is, I'm not particularly good at it. But as far as I can tell, no one else is either. O.K., sure, there are a handful of people I know who can play the game. But most of these guys got that way by neglecting every other responsibility they ever had, to spend the time it takes between tee and green to do so.

There are exceptions, of course. Not many, but they do exist. Take my friend, Bill. Bill is one of those annoying guys that can pick up anything requiring large amounts of physical dexterity and hand-eye coordination and master the better part of it in about seventeen seconds. You may have spent two years learning how to windsurf, and then Bill will drop by and say, "Hey, can I give it a try?"

He's pretty much got it on his second pass across the lake.

You've got to be good at biting your tongue with friends like Bill.

But he is the rare exception, far from the established rule. In fact, very few people on the planet can play the sport of Golf as it is designed to be played. Even the top fifty players in the world have lousy days on a fairly regular basis. Which is what makes the sport so great. You can have all the talent in the world and have practiced forty hours a week for the last twenty years, but if your heads not right, you're toast.

Whispering Loud and Clear

Tiger Woods seems to be the lone exception. A bad day for Tiger comes along about as often as a solar eclipse and has about the same duration. And all it really means is that he scores about like every other "professional" out there. When he's on, he smacks them by as much as fifteen strokes. (That's what he did in the U.S. Open this past week-end.) When he's off a bit, he beats them by two or three.

If you're not too familiar with how Golf is scored, let me clarify. Being beaten by fifteen strokes over seventy-two holes as a "Pro" is like running the 100-yard dash in the Olympics and having the other guy cross the finish line right about the time your heel comes out of the shadow of the starting block. i.e., you were never really in the game. Watching poor Ernie Els, arguably the second greatest golfer walking the planet, have to step up to the tee and hit behind Tiger was tough. You got the same sort of feeling you get for someone who has to stand up and give the announcements after the key note speaker has just finished. It makes you kind of nervous.

Golf, like most any sport, can teach you a lot about life, and it can do it in a lot of different ways. But I'm not going to repeat all the time-honored wisdom that true players of the game have written and spoken of so well over the years. If you want a good book that does so really well, read *A Fairway to Heaven; My Lessons from Harvey Penick on Golf and Life*, by Davis Love III. You can't go wrong.

A couple of weeks ago, however, I did witness an event that, while not on the golf course, did take place right next to it. I suspect that, for me, it will always be one of Golf's greater moments. It happened just before the start of this years "Lifeline Golf Tournament" to benefit the Roanoke Rescue Mission.

Perhaps the nicest thing about such tournaments is that they use a format known as "Captains Choice," which means you play the best shot that is made out of your foursome.

The Better Side of Golf

Wouldn't it be great if life were played more that way? That only our best efforts "counted?" And when we were out of sorts, or just not at our best, someone else was always available to pick up the slack? The boss stomps in and slaps a file down on your desk, "Revercomb—this story's garbage! What are you thinking about?"

"Jim, take it easy . . . use Tondalaya's article or something . . . it's Captain's Choice this week isn't it?"

No such luck. Golf may teach you quite a bit about life, but there are limitations.

This year's Rescue Mission Tournament began with the usual drill that has everyone report to their carts for the obligatory "giving of the rules" by the Tournament Director. Approximately Eighty of us had been assembled in two long rows of twenty carts each. The director was attempting to bring order to the group. Say all you want about cackling women at a bridge club or Junior League meeting, but quieting a group of eighty men in golf carts can be a fairly daunting task. It's just a hunch, but I don't think they have to use bull horns at the Junior League.

Once he had quieted the crowd, the director kept his commentary short, for his audience was clearly ready to get on with things. But just when it sounded like he was about to finish up, he hesitated and said, "I've got one more person who would like to speak to you today." There was a slight rise to the din of background conversation at this point. I remember thinking that if this guy wasn't quick, the director might have a mutiny on his hands.

A clean cut young man in his 30's walked purposely to the front of the two long rows of white carts. He cleared his throat and began.

"Good Morning," he said," My name is Deane Welch and I am an Alcoholic."

The bull horn was no longer needed. Eighty men went stone quiet.

Whispering Loud and Clear

Deane continued, "I began drinking in the eighth grade and my life pretty much slid downhill from there. By eighteen, I was drinking hard liquor and getting into a lot of things—including some scrapes with the law." His voice had a small twinge of emotion, but he was calm. There was the power of truth in his words, underpinned by the disarming effect of a bold confession.

"I lost jobs—I lost friends," he paused several moments and looked down, "I lost my family," he said.

He raised his eyes to meet ours.

"A couple of years ago I met a young girl who told me what the Rescue Mission was all about. I was skeptical and not real open to the idea. I had never had anyone speak to me about God before. But she didn't give up and ultimately she convinced me to go." He took a deep breath and raising his head slightly said, "I am a Christian now. I have been saved by Jesus Christ."

Every ear and every heart hung on his words and for a moment all you could hear was the rustle of the warm spring wind in the trees and the far-off call of a single songbird. The contrast of the lone man struggling up from the toughest rungs in life, standing in front of so many who seemed to have so much, was raised by the fact that I knew at least some of us out there in front of him had, or were, likely facing similar battles of alcohol or chemical dependency. You could feel the courageous words of this man working silently in those hearts, offering hope and promise and an unexpected blessing.

"I now work in the men's transient shelter," Deane continued. "It keeps me humble. Every day I am reminded of how easily life can get away from you. I try to take it one day at a time." Deane folded up the small white square of paper on which he had outlined his remarks and then said, "I want to thank all of you who help to support the Rescue Mission. They save a lot of lives down there." He then added

The Better Side of Golf

simply, "I know, because one of them was mine."

He nodded his appreciation for our attention and began to walk away, and as he did so 160 hands came together in support of his courageous comeback and honest testimony. One man with an exceptional heart left his group to go offer a thank you and a handshake of encouragement and support.

"To hell with the golf," I remember thinking. "This tournaments already won."

Such people are my biggest Heros—young men and women who have overcome the devil of addiction. It is so easy to be its slave with the long, hazy road wandering on seemingly eternal before you. The old addict suffers the burdens of habits that are long established, but the young one must confront the false notion that time is on his side and that he or she is too young to really be one anyways.

Remember my friend, Bill—the super coordinated guy that can do anything he sets his mind to? He was once enslaved to alcohol and its often life draining effects. In 1986 at age twenty-six, he put his last drink behind him and still does so one day at a time. He's now the Operations Manager for a division of a multinational corporation that does over Four Billion Dollars a year in business. Perhaps more importantly, like Deane, he's still helping others reclaim their own lives by leading twelve-step recovery groups and offering his own story to anyone, anytime.

Tiger Woods may play the best game of golf in the world, but I know of no one that plays a better game of life than people such as Deane and Bill.

Way to go guys. You inspire a great many more people than you realize.

10

The Goodness of Man

I had an interesting conversation with a friend the other day. It was one of those impromptu moments that come out of nowhere and never afford you the amount of time you would like to spend on the subject. We were just moments away from beginning an important meeting, and I had responded to one of his statements with what I felt was an innocuous "God willing."

"You and I may disagree on that . . . ," he responded.

"Disagree? Disagree on what?" I replied.

"The God thing." He said it rather quietly and in a tone that indicated that he wasn't sure if he really wanted anyone else to hear him. But he had said it, nevertheless. And he clearly wanted ME to hear it.

"Oh, that's O.K.," I replied. "We're all in different places along the journey." I offered it as one of those "shades of grey" responses that gives a nice easy way out, but also raises the question where "one is" and whether there is any "journey" occurring at all. If he was interested in continuing the dialogue, he still had a chance. He was.

"You and I are rather far apart actually," he responded.

"We are?" I replied.

"Yes—we are," he said, "I think I have a pretty good idea of what you believe, and all I can say is that I don't

. . . ," He paused a moment and then said rather emphatically, "I believe in the Goodness of man."

"So do I," I responded. "See, we're not that far apart." Now I was the one "taking the easy way out." The meeting was getting ready to begin and we both needed to have our wits about us. This wasn't the time or the place to take a deep theological dive. But he wasn't finished.

"No, I don't think so," he said. "I believe in the Goodness of man and that's pretty much it. Everything I do, I do for that reason and I live my life according to that principle." He paused a moment longer, and then said, "and I'm happy with that." But something in his voice wasn't completely convincing, and the fact that he wanted me to know his thoughts at all seemed to belie some element of doubt in them. I couldn't be sure, but it seemed like he was hoping for something in my answer. We didn't have time.

"Stay open", I responded, "You never know what the world might bring." I didn't really mean the world at all, of course, but rather God. But he knew what I meant. The meeting began at that moment and we haven't spoken of it since.

It has been several weeks since the conversation, and I have found myself repeatedly going back to the statement, "I believe in the Goodness of man." I have come up with about seventy-two books I would like my friend to read, but writings that have moved us to new understandings in our own lives, often don't connect with others as we might hope they would.

C.S. Lewis, however, had some powerful thoughts and reflections for such "moralists". Once a devout atheist, Lewis' own spiritual journey began in earnest as he wrestled with what he referred to as "The Law of Human Nature"— the idea that within the mind of all men there is a general idea of "right and wrong." Lewis contended that while we may define our ideals of "right and wrong" somewhat differently, we almost universally hold them to be true in one form or

The Goodness of Man

another. Where does such a notion come, from he wondered?

When this is understood in conjunction with the fact that none of us are particularly good at "practicing the kind of behavior we expect from other people"(living in accordance with our own ideas of "right and wrong"), Lewis felt that we had the cornerstones on which to build our understanding of ourselves and the universe.

"If men ought to be unselfish—ought to be fair", Lewis writes, "then this 'Rule of Right and Wrong' or 'Law of Human Nature' or whatever you want to call it, must somehow or other be a real thing—a thing that is really there and not made up by ourselves. It begins to look as if we shall have to admit that there is more than one kind of reality... that there is something above and beyond the ordinary facts of man's behavior and yet quite definitely real—a real law that none of us made, but which we find pressing on us."

And so according to one of the greatest thinkers of our time, Christian or otherwise, my friend was right, "the Goodness of man" does indeed exist—at least in so far as we understand that we feel an inexplicable and undeniable desire to live in accordance with it.

The question then seems to remain : Where does such Goodness come from? The random assemblage of carbon-based molecules that have somehow manifested themselves to articulate consciousness in the minds of men? Or the heart of a loving creator who breathes his very Spirit across the boundaries of time and space into a creation seemingly as fragile as the truth it seeks to understand?

Randomly or lovingly given we are at the very least free to answer as our souls see fit.

God descending as a man and dying withered and beaten on a cross to rise again in infinite Glory? In many ways it is the wildest and most "far fetched" of all our dreams and realities.

But if truth is invariably stranger than fiction, then I

Whispering Loud and Clear

suppose the greatest Truth of all isn't likely to come wrapped in brown paper and tasting like vanilla. Rather, it's more apt to be like the raspberry cream egg you once found in your Easter basket. All at once exotic and strange and desirable—and not at all what you thought it might taste like in the beginning. But it's likely the one you've never forgotten and somehow yearn to taste again.

Celebrate with joy and thanksgiving the "Goodness of man." The Goodness you are given in love.

11

An Unpaved Paradise

Last week I was spreading out some dirt along the alley in our back yard with the thought that I may one day need it for a parking pad. Unfortunately, it is a sort of "sacred spot"—set off and hidden by a short row of white pine trees on one side and a picket fence on the other that borders the alley. There is a low "dry stacked" stone wall beneath the pines and a Mulberry tree in the corner that helps shade the whole area. God speaks in such places, and the bright orange wild lilies growing along the fence in the corner seem to prove it.

The dirt was actually left over from a project at a neighbor's house. I had been shoveling for almost an hour and was just about through when a small, faded brown piece of plastic flipped up and out of the fertile black soil. I almost didn't notice it. It was the one-third remains of an ancient and long since canceled credit card. I wiped the layers of dirt away that concealed the raised letters and numbers beneath. At the top, the highly stylized cursive letters "SM" and part of an "A" could be seen. Beneath were the beginning of an account number—"6967-766..."

The name "Ms Martina Z..." was clearly visible at the bottom. I smiled at her memory. "Martina's 'Smartwear' card," I thought. "This hasn't seen the light of day for a while."

I never had a chance to know the "real" Martina. When my wife and I moved into our new home on Stanley Avenue in 1990 we had been married less than a week, and while Martina lived next door, our world was a million miles and more from hers. She lived with three of her five sisters, the youngest of which was perhaps in her late sixties at the time. The oldest was at least ninety, and I suppose Martina herself was in her mid to late seventies. She was already deep in the throws of Alzheimers at this point, and her sisters had to keep a fairly close watch on her.

This proved to be no easy task. Having grown up on Stanley Avenue (her father built their house in 1929), Martina was used to "going out," and it was not unusual to see her sneaking out of the house and wandering about our end of the block. The very first time I met her she had just pulled off one of her escapes. She approached me under our big Sugar Maple in the front yard. I had not yet been appraised of her condition.

"Good Afternoon," I said, wanting to make the best possible impression upon one of my new neighbors.

"They buried him here you know," came the reply.

"Excuse me?", I said.

"Yup, buried him here right underneath this tree . . . pretty much where you're standing." She pointed at my feet.

I was caught off guard to say the least. I stepped backwards onto our front walk so as not to desecrate the grave and looking down incredulously said, "Uh, . . . who, Uh . . . what . . . Uh, who did they bury here ma'am?"

"I'm not real sure," she replied, her lips tight and serious, "but they buried him here . . . that I know." She pointed again to the ground in the middle of the shade garden beneath the tree. "Right there."

"Oh," I said, thinking to myself that these were the things that must happen to all first time home buyers—unknown graves found in the front yard. My first call would

An Unpaved Paradise

be to that realtor . . . they were working for the other guy alright. Several awkward moments passed. At least for me.

"Uh, . . . I'm Stuart Revercomb," I finally said, extending my hand. "My wife and I just moved in a couple of days ago—I'm sure you noticed."

"I'm Martina, but everyone calls me Tini," she replied.

She paused a moment, and then with one hand cupped over the side of her mouth whispered dryly, "Don't worry, they buried him deep."

With that she walked back to the steps leading to her front porch, and with a glance over her shoulder to see if I were still watching, disappeared inside. I had laughed after her remark to indicate I understood her joke, but she had shown no change of emotion. I wondered if maybe she knew something the rest of us didn't.

I've been throwing a little extra mulch under that tree ever since.

Over the next several weeks I spied Martina picking up sticks in both her yard and ours. Often they were of the smallest variety, such that I began to question if perhaps she did suffer from some sort of dementia. The fact was finally confirmed when one of the other sisters asked if I had met her and then filled me in on her condition.

"Let us know if you ever see her out alone," she said. I replied that I would, but I remember thinking that if I did, I'd probably be calling a lot. So far "Tini" seemed to be pretty good at slipping past her guards.

As it turned out, I was right. I often found Martina out and about, either picking up all the sticks in the world or watching the birds fly from tree to tree in our back yards. Our conversations were always an adventure, but despite her often uncertain and confused state, she was able to give me a wonderful sense of what her life and her beloved neighborhood were like so many years ago. Not even all that Alzheimers could hide such a good and radiant soul.

Whispering Loud and Clear

But when she passed away in 1996, I was in many ways grateful she was free of a body that would no longer allow her to speak and live as herself. Her sisters still miss her dearly, but one of them remarked to me not too long ago that she knows, "Martina finally found her way 'Home'."

As I held that little piece of dirty plastic in my hand with the name etched partially at the base, I realized that I have incorporated much of her memory into my own sense of place—that the gangly old roses that cling to the rusty iron trellis and the mature Mulberry tree with its lilies beneath are as much mine now as they were once hers. And they are a large part of what makes this place we presently call "Home" something even more.

When the time comes, I don't think the kids will mind parking out front.

12

The Judge

One cold morning last February, while driving my son to school, I noticed a junk heap in front of a house about halfway up our block. Being woefully in possession of some sort of "junk recovery gene" (most likely from my father's side) I slowed down and gave the inauspicious collection of used housewares the old Revercomb, "there's got to be something worth saving in that pile of junk," scan.

You might say we refuse to refuse refuse.

"Look at all that great stuff," I thought, visually perusing the unwieldy collection—old lamps, broken bed posts, boxes of moldy books with delaminated covers, what to most folks of sound mind was little more than dispensable scrap. I had almost completed my scan and was easing into the accelerator when I saw it; there peeking out almost imperceptibly from behind a torn box of jumbled basement artifacts was a 1940's Emerson Electric tabletop fan. I backed up for a better look, but from the car it was still hard to tell what kind of shape it was in. I glanced at the clock. We were late for school. I'll give it a closer inspection when I get back, I thought.

Rifling through one's neighbor's junk collection on the curb can be somewhat embarrassing, but if it's done with the right combination of false indifference and nonchalance you can get away with it to the point of not appearing positively

Whispering Loud and Clear

destitute. The REAL embarrassment comes when you build up the courage, nay the audacity, to actually pull something out of the wretched pile to take home.

Such a move requires the confidence, composure and steely nerve of a master junk hound.

Offering a prayer that I was presently beholden only in the eyes of my Maker (who most certainly appreciates such efforts of salvation) I extricated the vintage fan from its grave by the curb and walked quickly toward home. I let it hang loosely from my side in an attempt to hide it from at least one side of the street and with the vain hope that by making the "effort look effortless," I was somehow lessening my culpability for such a desperate act. I reached the basement door and disappeared quickly inside.

It was here that I had the first real chance to behold my prize. It was American Engineering at its best. The motor housing was the unmistakable bullet shape of the 1940's and 50's, and the smooth sweeping curve of the pedestal base made it look as though it was a molded part of the surface upon which it sat. The grill was a wonderfully eclectic art-deco weave of galvanized wire that provided ample room to stick your whole fist through, and there was a cloth covered external electrical lead running from the base to the motor housing above.

One thing was certain. OSHA wasn't on the scene when they were building these babies.

The body was covered with some sort of greasy white film that had locked in what I figured was well over a half century of dust. But even in this condition you could sense something of the jet-black beauty that lay beneath. I gave the frayed and ragged cord a quick inspection and added a note for a new one on the "Lowe's List." I set the fan in an old clothes basket in my shop.

"Maybe I can get to it next week," I remember thinking wishfully.

The Judge

It is September and I have re-entered the shop for the 200th time since placing the old fan in the basket. I have just hung up the phone with one of my best friends. Broaddus Fitzpatrick's father, Judge Bev Fitzpatrick, is dying of cancer, and he has filled me in on what he can. The prognosis is not good. The Judge will not be with us much longer, he implies. We share a quiet moment over the phone, and I ask him to stop by tomorrow night for a glass of wine if he can make it. He says he'll try, but it will be hard—the whole family is spending most of their time by his side now.

Upon entering the shop, my eyes have once again fallen on the old fan now lying in two pieces connected by the wire between. It looks so hopeless and forlorn there, and for a moment I contemplate chucking the whole thing in the big rubber can in the corner. But something says, "Save it, don't give up on the old thing—there's still life there . . . don't give up."

I lift the skeletal remains and set it on the bench and begin searching for the new cord I purchased late last winter. My thoughts return to the Judge as I begin to disassemble and clean the old fan. It occurs to me that I am attempting to accomplish something that he himself loved to do—tinkering with old pieces of worn out machinery and restoring them to their original intended condition.

But the Judge didn't limit his restorations to just things. In fact his real focus was people, and he was one of the greatest healers of lives people around here have ever known. Much of it he did in his public life as a Judge by creating the "Honor Court"—a sentencing option he developed for alcoholics that gave them an honest opportunity at renewal when the rest of the world had given up on them. He did it as a servant in his church, teaching Sunday School classes to older youth and providing them with a perspective that many later said carried them through the most difficult years of their lives. He did it as a community volunteer leading the effort to save and renovate his abandoned old high school into the "Jefferson Center," which now houses community help organizations and various agencies for the arts. He did it as a father who, with his extraordinarily gracious wife Helen, raised three sons whose own contributions to their community are in many ways his greatest legacy.

And beyond this, and perhaps most importantly, he did it in ways you and I will never know: The phone call when the rest of the world had forgotten you—the supportive note or letter when you most needed the encouragement—the hearty joke that brought tears of laughter just when you thought you could no longer hold back the ones of sorrow—the well-placed greeting and the handshake that told you if all else failed you in this world there was one individual who really cared.

Such was the spirit of the man that left us in the quiet morning hours last Saturday.

I completed the restoration and reassembled the fan recently. Its outer parts are fresh and clean and oiled as factory new, but when I went to plug it in I had no idea what would happen. I was prepared for anything, including a shower of sparks, but as the copper prongs entered the outlet the old motor jumped to life and then quietly hummed along as though it had just been made. The breeze it moves is strong and sweet and it cools and comforts me now as I write this.

It's got a name. I call it the Judge.

13

It's Black and White

History brought us here. By no choice of our own, the events of the last couple of million years have conspired to bring us all to the point at which we presently find ourselves. Even at this moment, as you sit before an ether blue screen created by billions of atoms giving off the most minuscule amounts of photon energy, or hold in your hand a parchment that is the product of perhaps a century of photosynthesis by some unknown tree in an ancient forest, you are beholden to the past.

Unfortunately the actions of our species have not always been noble. Indeed the greed and avarice of mankind has written some pretty dark chapters for us—or perhaps better said, "into us." And no matter how hard we try to slip out from beneath the confining weight of their influence, we find ourselves trapped and struggling and laboring for air.

Consider the legacy of African slavery in the British Colonies that would one day become these United States of America. We can no more escape the reality of this wretched past than we can slip our own skin. It is part of us—an economic and social reality, against which anyone who happens to possess a bit more epidermal pigment than not, must struggle. But must we be conscripted to a stereotypical reaction to such a past?

Whispering Loud and Clear

The answer seems to be, only to the degree that we wish it upon ourselves.

It has been interesting to watch the unbiased reaction of my children to the differences among us that we refer to as "race." As my oldest son, George, experiences a widening world around him, meeting new friends at school, he often comes home and describes different aspects of their persons and personalities to us. Several of George's newfound friends are of African decent, but he has never used skin color to describe them unless he was going into detail and wanting us to know what they looked like. Skin color is just that—a physical trait bearing no relation to any other traits in his mind. People are either "dark skinned" or "light skinned" and that is that.

But history will surely catch him one day and plant the full grown tree of past wrongs in the untouched field of his memory. Its branches will be suspicion and fear and preconception and the wary distance that in many ways is a sort of "unconscious prejudice." Friends will be judged and denied inalienable rights because they are "black." Others will be threatened and accused falsely of denying the same because they are "white." The cycle of racial prejudice will surely continue and other biases will assault his view of the world around him.

I mourn the inevitability of such intrusions on the beauty of his young heart.

Lately, I have considered the notion that we are but one generation away from solving such problems. That if we could somehow start fresh and new with everyone born from this day forward as being somehow released from the cold boney grip of the past, we could create a world free of this and other historically supported ills.

We are told that God tried it once—finding one good man and wiping out the rest. It is assumed that he felt Noah's noble heart might sufficiently influence those to come. Needless to say, it proved to be a total failure. The creation found its way back to its previous way of thinking and doing things, and probably much faster than even God himself suspected it would. There's no reason to think that we would do otherwise today.

But perhaps an answer is closer than we might imagine. And perhaps it too comes as demonstrated by our very creator in the offering of himself in the kind of unconditional forgiveness that knows no boundaries and recognizes nothing of our fallen past. Is it possible for the human heart to emulate such forgiveness?

At times it appears so, but never on the scale and with the collective force that might somehow permanently overcome the centuries of injustice and hate among different races and ethnic groups.

Rather, it would appear that our only hope is by a slow and steady process whereby one heart at a time comes to new understandings through the particular circumstances and events of our own lives.

And not a little bit of Grace.

The next time you feel that stereotypical judgment rising up within you, or even the joke that offers the cheap laugh at another's expense, try and remember that such is the material by which our collective freedom from prejudice is lengthened. And by which others support far more radical views of intolerance.

If hearts need to change—let us start with our own.

14

It's a Willys Truck

As I mentioned in a previous article, "Cars I Have Known and Loved," I own a Chevy Tahoe. It is a wonderful combination of car and truck and rides better than my old Buick sedan. It has "on demand four wheel drive," a "five link coil spring suspension" and "hydroformed modular frame rails." There is a lot of new nifty sounding technology going on underneath all that sheet metal, and it's nice to have to be sure, but we're still getting to know each other. I still have to think to turn on the windshield wipers.

I also own a dark green 1961 Willys-Overland Pickup Truck. It's old and beat up, but strong and loyal and somehow . . . somehow, something more. If a piece of machinery can have a soul then this truck does, for it whispers quietly and eloquently all manner of truth. It takes me places no other vehicle can go—not even the Tahoe.

His name is Harvey—after his previous owner, his mechanic and the invisible Rabbit in the movie of the same name. It's certainly not a normal name for a truck. Most men name equipment, be it ship or plane or old truck, for women of note. But Harvey is not feminine. He's muscular and tough and he wants to work. He's a "1 Ton" and last year when I overloaded him with a ton and a half of old brick in the bottom of our recently excavated new basement, several

Whispering Loud and Clear

of the younger construction workers chuckled.

"He'll never get that thing out of there," they jeered.

Rodney, the older driver of the loader that had done the excavation, thought otherwise. He laid back in the big black seat of his Caterpillar earthmover and said, "That there's a Willys boys . . . day in the park for that thing . . . he'll be fine."

I shifted Harvey into 4 wheel low and he crept out of that hole like an M1 Abrahms Tank.

"Son of a . . . ," one of the young men remarked as we passed them.

"That's a helluva truck," said another.

Rodney smiled and nodded atop his big yellow loader.

Harvey ignored them all—grinding his way to the top of the hill, making me look like I knew what I was doing, which I didn't.

"Thank you," I said to Harvey as we turned up the alley.

The 38-year-old low range gear box whined his reply, "Anytime sir. I'm built to serve."

He is built to serve, but he's not built for speed. Harvey's max is about 62 MPH. That's downhill, with a tail wind, in thin air, with the windows up. His normal maximum cruising speed is closer to 60 MPH, and even then you better drop him down to 45 every so often. This lack of modern speed makes getting out on the interstate a little intimidating because the rest of the world goes flying by you on the left in a maddening rush. By refusing to join them, Harvey offers a fresh perspective on the pace of our frenetic culture.

From Harvey's cab it's clear that most of us rush right past the more meaningful moments in life. Ever forward we go, our hands tight upon the wheel, eyes narrowed and transfixed on the asphalt or the cars before us. We sail around one another to be the first to the ramp, feeling victorious when we have put the rest of the world behind us, and frustrated when someone else has "won."

Cruising along with Harvey the breeze passes through

It's a Willys Truck

and the head clears and you notice so many little things you hadn't before . . . a doorway with an old man and a child within—a garden with a row of blooming pear trees at the end—a flock of birds landing in a spring green field. You find yourself wishing everyone else would slow down just a little, if not for a moment. But the world just keeps sailing by in the "passing lane." Perhaps we pass more than each other when we're in it.

Harvey has never said too much about this behavior, but I get the feeling it upsets him. "It wasn't always this way," he once told me as a little red sedan shot by in the middle lane. But if over-hurried drivers get him down, there is one thing that is sure to pick him up.

Snow.

Harvey is never happier than when it snows. His absolute favorite thing to do is load the kids up in the back with their sleds and haul them to the top of our hill on Stanley Avenue. He drops them off and then putters around the long way to the bottom to pick them all up again. His wipers loosely slap the glass in rhythm, and his defroster motor sings an aging tune, but he's as happy as the day he was made. When we finally come in for cocoa and a fire, Harvey sighs to a stop and his headlights cry little rivulets of water from the melting snow on his hood.

I am absolutely certain that they are tears of Joy.

Late at night on such days when the children have all gone to bed, Harvey often takes me for a ride to the top of the hill. He burbles quietly along past the sleeping houses as the snow floats lazily down around the street lights. We meet others at the top and sip beer and smoke cigars, as the lights of the city fade in and out of view beneath us. Invariably someone asks what year Harvey is and I get to respond, "1961—He was made the same year I was." It makes me feel good somehow to say so.

But while we are the same age, we are also different of

Whispering Loud and Clear

course. For Harvey, being a machine, is always no more or less than who he was created to be. And by virtue of this, he is able to fulfill his calling and carry out his mission as long as his parts will allow.

I, on the other hand, am still becoming who I am—am still on the assembly line—and whether I like it or not, I am shaped by the influence of the world around me. In my rare and better moments I am like Harvey—true to who I was created to be—shaped only by my Creator and willing when I am called to serve.

In my lessor ones I am something else altogether.

I love that old truck. He takes me places no other vehicle can go.

15

Just a Coincidence

Sometimes God can't help but be obvious in order to save us from ourselves. Sometimes he must surely squint his all seeing eyes, and holding his holy breath, allow grace to work itself out in the full light of human consciousness.

Sometimes he must allow a coincidence to occur.

We have all experienced them, great and small—sometimes seemingly pointless and often even silly and awkward in their simplicity. But other times they are remarkable and beyond our ability to fathom. A coincidence can point to something wondrous and inspiring and true—reaffirming in our seeking hearts something of the "great mystery" in which we move and breathe and live our lives.

Not long ago, I was building a fence and needed one more two-by-four to complete the last section and "re-close" the yard. In many ways, it represented the final act of a year long renovation process that included adding a fairly large addition to our house. I sorted through the few odd length boards I had left and lifted one up to measure it between the post and the new shed wall to which it would be attached. It was the exact length I needed—making a perfect fit to within a sixteenth of an inch when placed in the "final gap."

I had still been wrestling somewhat with our decision to

Whispering Loud and Clear

add on, hoping that we had made the right call in renovating as opposed to moving to a larger house. This remarkable "perfect fit" on the last board seemed to be the "whisper" I needed.

A couple of years earlier as part of a "Pastoral Nominating Committee" for our church, I was surprised to see an application with the name "George Anderson"on it. It was the name of my great-grandfather as well as my first son—George Anderson Revercomb. "Wouldn't that be something if HE turned out to be the guy," I remarked to the committee one night early in the process. Over two years, 200 applications and numerous weekend trips later, we called one George C. Anderson to the pulpit of Second Presbyterian Roanoke.

But not before one of our Committee members laughingly remarked one night, "Here's a resume from a guy that lives on an interesting street . . . "George Anderson Lane."

Whack us over the head with a perfect fitting two-by-four why don't you.

Carrying his little joke one step further, the Holy Spirit arranged for a house to come on the market right next to ours at the perfect moment that the Right Reverend Anderson and his brood were seeking to move from Mississippi.

"I'm not sure WHAT I think about living next door to a minister," I told him, "Much less my own."

"You?!" Anderson replied, "Now you'll know who I REALLY am!"

Two days after moving in I caught him flying paper airplanes off his porch roof to the neighborhood kids below. I knew who he was alright, and coincidence or not, he and his family would be a perfect fit in the gap on Stanley Avenue.

Sometimes such moments don't offer the kind of immediate clarity we might hope for, but their providential goodness seems apparent enough. Such was the case in 1980 as

Just a Coincidence

several of us milled around in the shell-covered driveway of a South Carolina beach house after a "post high school graduation week." The cars were all packed and we were attempting to say goodbye to several friends whom we knew we might not see for a very long time.

Most of us were more than a little bleary eyed after seven endless nights of teenage celebration and revelry. Our wallets didn't look so strong either. We were, for the most part, flat broke. I stood barefoot in the drive counting change with my two riding partners, Bill and Big Al. Would eleven dollars and three-quarters of a tank of gas get us back to Roanoke? We were hoping so.

As we concluded our deliberations, I notice out of the corner of my eye what appeared to be a dollar bill blowing across the sandy flat next to the side of the house. No one seemed to be in pursuit.

"Wow, we could sure use that," I thought, as I began to gingerly step among the sand burrs to go retrieve it. I must have looked like a desperate refugee crossing a mine field as I "ouched" and "expleted" my way over the tiny round sand thistles. I pondered going back for a moment, but that buck might just mean a couple of hamburgers in Rockingham.

I persevered, but just as I came upon it a gust of wind blew it from beneath my grasp. I probably would have turned back then, but I was sure I had seen a corner that had both a "1" and a "0" in it. "Hey guys, I think it's a Ten!" I bellowed across the dune I was now scaling.

"Riiiight!"came the not so believing reply.

Forgetting my throbbing feet, I took three more quick steps and pounced on the wayward green tumbleweed. I jumped up and holding it high as I looked back to the skeptical gallery, declared, "SEE, I TOLD YOU . . . IT'S A TE . . . " I hesitated. There was another zero in back of the first one.

"Son of a.. . . IT'S A HUNDRED!!!" I yelled.

"Revercomb, come off that dune and quit playing around with that buck . . . we've gotta go . . . "

"NO JOKING GUYS . IT'S A HUNDRED SOMO-LIANS . . . LOOK!!!"

My enthusiasm quelled their skepticism. They began to squint their eyes in an effort to see the number. As I approached the car with the bill in my teeth, their mouths began forming big sagging "O"s. No one else claimed it. I was the hero of the hour. Lunch and a little "high test" were on me.

Later that day my friends and I would encounter torrential rainstorms across the Piedmont of North Carolina. And just south of Greensboro in the heart of the worst storm cell, as day faded to night, the wipers on my 1972 Pontiac would give out completely. Thanks to the $100.00 bill we were able to consider the possibility of stopping at a hotel for the night, which we wisely did. I can say with great certainty that without it our daring young minds would have journeyed on, wipers or not.

We arrived home the next morning to the news that one of our schoolmates had been killed the night before when the car he was riding in skated off a rain-soaked road in Roanoke. It wasn't long before that $100.00 bill and the opportunity it later provided to stop in the midst of the darkening storm, seemed more blessing than coincidence.

Over the years I have come to the conclusion that such moments of coincidence are, even at their simplest, more than we would readily laugh them off to be. That a "coincidence" might best be seen as an echo of hope returning back to the heart of faith from some distant and eternal place—an occurrence when the subtle voice of creation is somehow less hidden in the details of our lives.

Writer Frederick Buechner has a wonderful perspective. A coincidence he says, "is a whisper from the wings that goes something like this: You've turned up in the right place

Just a Coincidence

at the right time. You're doing fine. Don't ever think you've been forgotten."

Try to remember that the next time the vending machine is all out of your favorite drink but you get one anyway when you press the other button. Or you see the name of a town where you have just accepted a new job spelled out on a license plate on the car in front of you.

Just a coincidence?

Maybe.

Or maybe not.

"Wishful Thinking: A Theological ABC"
New York: Harper & Row, 1973

16

Thanks for the Memories
(Most of Them Anyway)

I awoke this morning to the following headline: "Your Mind Starts Going In Your 20's, Studies Find." Slow news day, huh.

Twenties?? I had come to the conclusion that mine had started slipping at about age seven when a very persuasive teacher convinced me for a brief period of time that math was somehow "fun."

There is, of course, nothing fun about math. Math stinks. But for a while there I searched pretty hard for the "fun" in it. I think I came close once counting my Halloween candy, but I lost my concentration somewhere around eighty pieces and was never able to reestablish an accurate tally. I guess the voters down in Florida know what I'm talking about.

At age fourteen, in a further indication that my faculties were beginning to leave me at an alarming rate, I began to accept the possibility that maybe girls didn't have "cooties" after all, and somewhere around the age of seventeen, I got the nerve to actually ask one out. We went to dinner and a movie and dessert after that, and then I took her home and she said, "Thank You" and closed the door.

I recall being out about twenty-five bucks and having not

much more to show for it than the memory of some really awkward moments of silence. I continued to ask girls out every six months or so with similar results, which pretty much substantiates the contention that by one's twenties we are mostly out of our minds. In fact, I can recall some moments in college between the age of nineteen and twenty-three that it was quite debatable that I had any brain at all. Perhaps it's best if we don't highlight such memories here.

I know my mom will be happy with that decision.

I chose to read this morning's article even though I knew there was little likelihood that I would remember a single word by lunch time. To my surprise, the German scientist who conducted the various studies and tests in support of the theory also came to the conclusion that older people compensate for memory loss with "the increased knowledge and wisdom that they have garnered over the years."

My only question is how does one use "increased knowledge and wisdom that is garnered over the years" if what is "garnered" is mostly forgotten beginning in one's twenties?

Wasn't that his first point?

I guess I never was very good at Science either.

My 97-year-old Grandmother has little memory of the "average" or more difficult moments of her life or even the ones five minutes ago that aren't in some way remarkable. But she can tell you all about the moment she first met my Grandfather. Or about the time in 1921, in rural Pennsylvania before it was "appropriate" for women to drive, that she tucked her hair up under her father's hat and drove her four sisters to the State Fair two counties away.

She remembers with a guilty laugh the strange look on the young policeman's face as they motored through the front gate. She tells me she remembers that face like it was yesterday. She also remembers that the parking brake was extremely hard to release.

I'm thankful that God has given her such memories to

Thanks for the Memories

keep and to share, and equally thankful that she has forgotten a great many more. For if we're honest with one another, we'll admit that a large part of our lives just aren't worth remembering. Either we ourselves, or those we love, or the world around us has let us down in some sad way, and if we were somehow forced to hang on to such moments we would surely one day perish beneath them.

Perhaps, of all the things we should be "thankful for," is the promise that there is a God who has separated us from the painful memories that might otherwise haunt our past—and who in turn has freed us to the hope and potential of a limitless future with him.

Thanks be to God indeed—for all we do, and do not have.

17

Jerry Rice Figures It Out

I have never been a Jerry Rice fan. Probably because he's just too darn good.

For those of you who haven't seen a Pro Football game in twenty years and don't plan on it for another twenty, let me explain that Jerry Rice is simply the best Wide Receiver to ever play the game.

Rice holds the following records:

Career touchdowns, Career receiving touchdowns, Career receptions, Career receiving yards gained, Season receiving yards, Season receiving touchdowns, Seasons with 50+ receptions, Seasons with 100+ receptions, Game receiving touchdowns, Games with 100+ receiving yards, Consecutive 1,000 yard seasons, Consecutive games with a reception, Consecutive games with a TD reception, Consecutive post season games with a reception, 49ers most career points, MNF most touchdowns, Pro Bowl Consecutive visits, Pro Bowl total visits, Pro Bowl 1995-1996 MVP, Super Bowl points in a game, Super Bowl TDs in a game, Super Bowl reception TD's in a game, Super Bowl receptions in a game, Super Bowl receiving yards in a game, Super Bowl fastest touchdown, Super Bowl career TD's, Super Bowl career receptions TD's, Super Bowl career points, Super Bowl career receiving yardage, Super

Whispering Loud and Clear

Bowl career combined net yardage . . . etc., etc., etc . . .

If I were to list the things in which he is listed as number two you'd be flipping pages until next Thursday, but you get the picture—the guy is All World, All Galaxy, All Universe and beyond. But I still don't like him. It's hard to like a guy that good. Even if he did come from some no-name college, and is known to have outworked every other player in the league to get where he is today.

My apologies to all you "Mississippi Valley State" grads out there. Truthfully, I figure the odds of an honest-to-goodness MVS grad reading this article are about as good as my getting back up on the gutters to take the Christmas lights down this week. But if you are, let me know and I'll eat my hat on national television. And I'll do it while singing the praises of old Mr. Rice.

Recently in an interview, Rice was asked to remember his favorite moment in football—the highlight of his extraordinarily brilliant career. Was it one of the playoff touchdowns that took them to their first Superbowl? Was it a game winning Superbowl touchdown itself? Or perhaps it was one of his other 1214 gravity-defying catches that seem to be part of every NFL highlight film ever made?

Nope, none of the above.

When asked, Rice responded that while he couldn't remember the exact game or even the year it took place, his favorite moment of his extraordinary career was throwing a block that sprung Quarterback Steve Young for a touchdown.

What?? The most prolific receiver to ever play the game remembers a block for another player above all else? It says something about Rice, to be sure, but perhaps it says something about the rest of us as well.

In considering the noted and not so noted careers of both family and friends, especially those who have already retired, it occurs to me that often what we do the least is what we value the most. Serving others in some special way

86

seems to be what all of us, sooner or later, refer to as being "what life is all about," and what we should be "all about" as well.

• A Heart Surgeon, who through years of training and the skill of his hands has saved thousands of lives, remembers more fondly the moments when he was able to successfully offer comfort to the grieving family of the patient that didn't pull through.

• The Judge whose rulings have changed the lives of countless individuals remembers most dearly the moment his family sacrificed their own Christmas to come to the aid of another family whose father the Judge himself had just been forced to place behind bars.

• The Grocery Store Manager who sacrifices his own time with family by staying late through the holidays preparing special orders so that others can enjoy their own holiday traditions. He might not yet confess it, but there will come a day when these will be some of his "favorite" memories.

Why is that? Why do we most remember "blocking for the other guy" among all the events of our own "stellar careers"—whatever it is that we do?

It is because, when all is said and done, the Savior who's birth we celebrate every December twenty-fifth, had it right. We truly are "built to serve." The problem is we just have a hard time remembering it. Or as my 3-year-old would say, "I have a hard time knowing that, Dad . . . "

I have a hard time "knowing it" too, but every now and then, by Grace, I seem to catch at least a glimpse of what I think both Jerry and Jesus are talking about.

May the coming years bring you plenty of catches and touchdowns, and the "blocks" that last a lifetime.

18

Goodbye Sweet Abbey

I had a pretty good column lined up for today. It was a happy affair, involving an extraordinary day in the life of my son George, which happened to occur on his 8th birthday. It is positive and upbeat and full of joy because that's what that day was all about. But it will have to wait until next week, because today our home is in mourning. We have lost our beloved dog, Abbey.

Abbey was an SPCA special—a true "American." An amalgamation of God only knows how many dogs, but primarily shepherd and collie with maybe a hint of malamute—more commonly known amongst mixed-breed dog lovers as a "black and tan."

We called her "The Ab-Dog." And she was something very special.

My wife and I acquired Ab-Dog long before we acquired the four children. She was our first born, and being such, became the dog we "practiced on." If you can't raise a dog half decent, we decided, then maybe we would forgo having children altogether. But the Ab Dog turned out O.K. and we went on from there. And so did Abbey. Over the last ten years she has helped us in no short measure raise and rear our children—not so much in any "heroic" way, as just being there for them and us, day in and day out to play and to greet and to comfort and to love.

Although I suppose it is inevitable, I cannot imagine our memories of her ever fading—the way she sometimes slept on her back with all four paws pointing up and bent at the wrists as though she were jumping a hedge row but upside down—training the children to walk, by letting them hold on to her back and then leading them to the cabinet where the dog treats were—greeting us every day in the driveway as though we had been gone for six months—letting out a soft moan from the foot of our bed when the night was cold . . .

A dog like Abbey that becomes part of your family is a part of the everyday of your life—a part of you, really, and the relationships you have with those you love most. For those who have lost such animal loved ones, you know what I am talking about. For those that haven't, I don't imagine there are words that can describe it.

Suffice to say that such animals have it within their beautiful souls to love almost completely unconditionally—something the vast majority of the rest of us have a pretty hard time doing. The gift of their life is in the giving of themselves, wherever and whenever needed, and without thought or hesitation. They simply love. And they give their love simply.

Call me blasphemous if you want to, and they are only animals I know, but it is a heart like Christ they possess.

We buried Abbey yesterday in our back yard, up in back of the pines under which she used to lay so often. We did so as a family with the exception of two year old Rob, whom we knew wouldn't grasp what we were doing. We read the Twenty-Fourth Psalm because it speaks of the fullness of the earth and all who dwell in it. And then the Twenty-Third Psalm, because we needed the comfort. After a prayer of thanks for the gift of her life, we gently placed her in the grave with her tags and a tennis ball. The children each

Goodbye Sweet Abbey

added a "milk bone," and then we said goodbye.

The night passed slowly, and the morning sun did not bring with it quite the relief or "progress" my wife and I had hoped for. The children were thankfully much better, however, and were generally able to hit the ground running, as the promise of a new day and an endless summer lay like a mirage before them.

But the morning was not without its own whispers for us.

Shortly after everyone took off for swim practice I ventured into our upper yard to retrieve a sprinkler and check the spot where we buried her. I noticed that I had left the Bible we used in our small service yesterday on the fence that runs along the back of our property. The morning was bright and glorious—the slanting rays of the sun penetrating through the branches of a mulberry tree to the hallowed ground below. The singing of the birds seemed especially vibrant.

I flipped the Bible openly randomly. It fell to Psalm 148.

> Praise the LORD from the heavens, praise him in the heights above.
> 2 Praise him, all his angels, praise him, all his heavenly hosts.
> 3 Praise him, sun and moon, praise him, all you shining stars.
> 4 Praise him, you highest heavens and you waters above the skies.
> 5 Let them praise the name of the LORD, for he commanded and they were created.
> 6 He set them in place for ever and ever; he gave a decree that will never pass away.
> 7 Praise the LORD from the earth, you great sea creatures and all ocean depths,
> 8 lightning and hail, snow and clouds, stormy winds that do his bidding,
> 9 you mountains and all hills, fruit trees and all

Whispering Loud and Clear

cedars,
10 wild animals and all cattle, small creatures and
flying birds,
11 kings of the earth and all nations, you princes
and all rulers on earth,
12 young men and maidens, old men and children.
13 Let them praise the name of the LORD, for his
name alone is exalted; his splendor is above
the earth and the heavens.
14 He has raised up for his people a horn, the
praise of all his saints, of Israel, the people
close to his heart. Praise the LORD.

"Let THEM praise the name of the Lord," the Psalmist
writes.
Let them indeed—including sweet Abbey.

New International Version (NIV)
Copyright 1973, 1978, 1984 by The International Bible Society

19

Big George's Day of Grace

Do you remember the kind of desire you used to have as a child? I mean REAL desire: the kind that became such a preoccupation that nothing could distract you from it—the kind that was like a sort of "cellular thirst" where every cell in your body screamed for the object of your desire—the kind you used to get with the Sears and Roebuck catalogue on the living room floor in early December. If you remember that kind of desire, then you know how badly my son George has wanted a turtle this summer.

Such was the depth of his longing, that when we planned a camping trip in June on the Cow Pasture River, we made the focus of the expedition a turtle hunt for George. As soon as we exited the Interstate and headed into the countryside, he and sister, Gussie, began to scan the sides of the road for some sign of a wayward terrapin. It didn't take long to find one. The only problem was that it was the car in front of us. The guy was maintaining a melancholy 47 MPH in a posted 55. As soon as we came to the first clear passing zone, I moved out to pass. 50-55-60-65 . . . we passed the vehicle quickly in order to get back in our lane before the dotted line turned solid. It was about the time we crossed it that I saw the drab brown Allegheny County Sheriffs's cruiser backed up against some bushes along a railway trestle.

Whispering Loud and Clear

We sailed by at a cool 68 MPH.

My Ray Bans met his as the lights came on. "Of all the rotten luck," I thought . . . "Maybe he'll let me off since I was passing that guy." But something told me it was unlikely. I advised the children what was about to happen. There was great excitement as they had never done this before. They both beamed like Cheshire cats out the back window as the officer came on in hot pursuit.

"Dad, are we ALL going to jail or just you?" Gussie asked matter of factly.

The officer was professional and courteous, but he wasn't forgiving. "That's 71 in a 55, Mr. Revercomb. If you don't wish to pay it out of court, you need to be at the Covington Court House on July Nineteenth—Circuit Court—First Floor."

"Hey! That's my birthday!" George excitedly offered. The officer smiled as he walked away.

"Thank you," I said.

I hate it when I thank a Policeman for a ticket.

The rest of the trip went much better. In fact, it was a glorious weekend for camping, with lots of fishing and river-rafting and snorkeling. But there weren't many turtles to be had. George's cousin, James, did spot a whopper of a snapping turtle living under a ledge about eight feet below the river's surface. As soon as the question was out of George's mouth I gave him a firm answer:

"George, your Dad is safely on the surface and that two-foot wide snapper is eight feet under right where he should be, and ne'er the twain shall meet," I said.

"What's 'twain' mean Dad?" George asked.

"No turtle," I replied.

As the weeks passed George eventually resigned himself to never finding a turtle. He did keep a line of his prayers dedicated to finding one, however, so I knew the desire was still there.

In the meantime, I had decided not to pay the ticket out

of court. I had three reasons:

1. I had never seen the Courthouse in Covington where my Grandfather once practiced law and where my Dad's Cousin, Roscoe Stephenson of Virginia Supreme Court fame, once sat on the Bench.

2. I wanted eight-year-old George to get an idea how our legal system works.

3. I wanted to see if the law would differentiate between someone cruising happily along at 71 MPH and a driver who had jumped up to that speed to get back in a lane safely while passing.

When my name was called, I gave all three reasons to the judge exactly as you see them above. I told him I was as guilty as the day was long and that the officer at hand was as professional as they come, but I did give the word "differentiate" a good bit of emphasis. The judge rubbed his chin for several moments. George watched curiously from the gallery.

"Of course the law differentiates . . . ," he finally said rather exasperated. "I tell you what, do one session of a driver improvement class and I'll drop the charge . . . How's that sound?"

"Reasonable enough," I responded.

"Send me the certificate when you're done," he said looking over his glasses.

"Yes Sir," I replied.

We decided to celebrate our big legal victory with a glass of chocolate milk at the "Club Car" in Clifton Forge, where we also picked up some sandwiches for lunch. It was here that our day began to gather some very positive momentum. Before leaving town we browsed a small antiques shop a couple of doors down from the Club Car.

Whispering Loud and Clear

George spotted a stack of something halfway back and moments later came up with an antique NFL platter that featured all the old team's helmets on it.

"HOLY COW DAD—LOOK AT THIS!" he exclaimed loud enough for the store's owners to hear him. There would be no dickering on the $8.00 price tag.

We took our newfound treasure and headed down Route 220 towards "Roaring Run"- a National Park location just outside of Fincastle Virginia, where we had decided to have our lunch. As we passed the Gala Natural Gas Substation, we noticed an archeological dig going on and pulled off the side of the road to investigate. The scientists were carefully exhuming the remains of a 1200-year-old Indian tribe. One of them stopped to give us a fifteen minute tutorial. George and I were enthralled. It was like being on the set of a National Geographic documentary. The day just kept getting better.

When we arrived at "Roaring Run," we made our way down to a large rock in the middle of the stream that runs directly in front of the 100-year-old Iron Ore Furnace that still stands at the site. The air was cool and verdant among the moss covered rocks and fast moving water. We talked and laughed and had our fill. Things were going so well that we decided to look for a turtle. We didn't find one, but we did find an incredible blackberry patch. George thought it would be best if we left them for the bears.

On the way out, I slowed down at the entrance to the park and contemplated going back the way we had come. But somehow that didn't feel quite right. "Let's keep going forward," I said. We took a right turn towards "Oriskiney."

A couple of miles later George brought the turtle up again. He started telling me something about what turtles liked and how they were around with the dinosaurs and where they were likely to be found on a day like today. I was half-listening looking out over the rolling farmland as we eased around a bend in the road when, boom—one of those moments hit that

Big George's Day of Grace

makes you feel as though you must be dreaming. There in the middle of the road with his head arched high and his legs fully extended was the most glorious Box Turtle you have ever seen. I had just enough time to bring the car to a stop.

George's mouth was drawn in a big oval. His eyebrows angled up like a porch roof. We both sat there staring out the window incredulously.

"That's a turtle," I finally said.

George turned his head and stared at me a moment. Then his face became one big smile. We both jumped out of the car and ran toward the turtle who beat a hasty retreat back inside his home. We did too, but not before driving across a shallow stretch of a nearby river and exploring the area around Oriskiney.

That afternoon George had six friends coming for a Birthday sleep-over. We went to see the movie "Cats and Dogs" and then went out to dinner at a Chinese restaurant that only the "old man" knew about. The boys howled with laughter at the movie, and the "Pu-Pu Platters" were quite the hit at "Fiji." The day just couldn't get better for George.

But the night could.

To entertain (and wear out) the boys, I had planned a nighttime "flashlight" hike up the old road that winds up the front of Mill Mountain. As we rounded the turn two-thirds of the way up, we ran into Mayor Ralph Smith who was just coming out of his house. I hailed Ralph and asked him if he would mind greeting George and his friends on his special day. Ralph's eyes beamed when I asked him. "Send them on over," he said with a smile. The boys might as well have been meeting the President. They nervously stood at attention as George introduced himself.

"I-I-I'm George Revercomb," he said shakily.

"Well George, it's so very nice to meet you," Ralph said humbly. "Is it really your birthday today?"

"Yes sir," George replied.

Whispering Loud and Clear

"I bet you couldn't guess when my birthday is?" said Ralph.

"No, I'm sure I couldn't," George responded sheepishly.

"Today," said Ralph with a grin. George looked like he'd just won a Noble Prize.

"You're kidding?" Said George.

"No, I'm not," said the Mayor. "C'mon boys," said Ralph, "I've got something for you." A few minutes later they were all having cake with the Mayor on his terrace overlooking the lights of the city.

That night when I went down to the basement to check on the boys, I found George lying awake in his sleeping bag among his slumbering friends. "Animal Planet" flickered quietly on the TV in the corner. I crawled over top of the conflagration of puffy bags to say goodnight.

"I hope you had a good birthday," I whispered, unable to contain a smile that gave away my happiness for him.

George paused for several seconds and then without breaking his eyes from the ceiling, said with a grin, "Probably the best day of my life Dad."

I wanted to ask if he remembered the disappointment of the camping trip in June, and how the ticket that had seemed like such a bad thing at the time, had ultimately led us to what we had hoped for all along. I wanted to ask him if he had felt the Grace of the day as it had unfolded, and if the sheer joy of so many unexpected good turns coming on his birthday had made his heart leap as it had mine.

But I didn't. I could see it playing out in his eyes as he stared at the flickering ceiling, and I knew that things discovered and contemplated on our own have a way of staying with us in ways that a parent can never teach. I kissed him good night and turned off the T.V. and started up the darkened steps. As I got to the top of the stairs, I heard George whisper softly, "Thanks Dad."

If I've had a better day, I can't remember it.

20

Fish of Grace: Jim's Fish

My first "Fish of Grace," must have been the very first one I caught. My Dad took my brothers and me fishing as often as he could, and some of my fondest memories are of being with them while walking the banks of a nearby stream or plying the waters of some distant lake while camping. They were and are the moments I have been closest to them, and I feel certain, we all to each other.

There is something about being on the water in the common pursuit of such an illusive and beautiful creature that brings men closer. I'm not sure entirely why . . . there just is. Christ came to his Disciples several times while fishing. To me it is no surprise.

In the next three stories I will try to convey something of three separate moments, when in addition to all the glory that nature can provide on any given day, something even more was realized; when God seemed to speak out of what might have been just another ordinary moment in some otherwise ordinary lives . . . and more than just a fish was brought in.

The first such fish would belong to my brother, Jim, who's ability with all manner of fishing gear seems to come as naturally to him as, well—a fish to water. Jim was "born to fish" and one glorious day in Montana, while on a trip with my other brother, Randy, and my Dad, we were given the honor of witnessing a moment that would forever substantiate this reality.

The trip had gone famously. We had stayed at a ranch that specialized in feeding its patrons well and providing the kind of guides capable of taking its guests to places where the fish would do the same. We floated "the Snake," fished the Green River and found great success on several nearby creeks and runs that flowed from the Rockies like so many picture post card streams that might be imagined while walking dehydrated through the desert.

You might say that as long overdue fishermen go, our thirsts were well assuaged.

But the highlight of the trip came near the end of the last day as Dad, Jim, Randy and I explored a small stream not more than a mile from the lodge where we were staying. As usual, we all started out fairly close to each other but far enough away that the long curves of our probing lines would not become entangled. Jim was opposite me on the other side of the stream and down about fifty yards to my left. Dad was just upstream from him on my right, and brother Randy was opposite him on my side working his way up river.

With the exception of Jim, our casting styles were more or less the same, varying only in small ways that seemed to reflect our personalities. Dad was steady and methodical and watchful. Not so much full of anticipation, as ready and willing when the "moment" came. Brother Randy was deliberate and purposeful and aggressive. If the fish hit, he would do well with the setting of the hook. He wasn't so much patient as persistent, working the same hole continually until any reasonable chance of success had been exhausted. I was somewhere in-between, focused upon the task at hand but also capable of being distracted by a passing bird or even the unusual shape of a scudding cloud in the deep blue Montana sky.

Fish of Grace: Jim's Fish

Brother Jim's casting reflected something else entirely. It was balance and purpose and rhythm and confidence all rolled into one motion, and he offered it with a feather light ease that stood out against our journeymen efforts. There was no work to the motion. The rod and line became a natural extension of his small frame, and the minuscule fly was always presented at the end of the "tippet" with such deftness and touch that rarely a ripple was seen.

It was on just such an easy and graceful display that the fish rose cautiously to meet him.

"Zzzzzzzzzzzip," Jim's line sang through his reel as he brought tension to the strike and rocked back in his stance. It was immediately clear this was not one of the run-of-the-mill Cutthroat Trout that we had been catching all week. His rod bent wildly toward the water and Jim was forced to give the powerful fish a great deal of line.

"Uh, . . . think I've got something down here . . . " It was all he ever said as he began what developed into an epic battle between a devoted fisherman who had patiently waited for an opportunity to test his skills and a fish that seemed determined to confound them all.

For more than twenty minutes Jim fought the massive Cutthroat—at one point being cajoled, then guided and then literally pulled beneath a small stone bridge and down across some shallow but fast moving water. He battled the huge "cutty" further through some small rapids and ultimately made his stand along a low swale of gravel about 100 yards from where the journey began. He landed the fish smoothly, netting it cleanly from beneath and with a smile as wide as the western sky, paused briefly for a picture before easing the trophy back into the ice cold water. Its emerald green back and speckled silver sides disappeared like a mirage into the bottom of the river and in a flash it was gone.

I swear to you that it was not entirely unlike the scene in

Whispering Loud and Clear

"A River Runs Through It," where the younger son catches his glorious prize and is swept down the river. Like the extraordinary scene in the movie, this was an opportunity Jim had longed for over the years. It had eluded him, but now it had arrived at the perfect moment like a benediction over all his efforts. I couldn't help but remember the endless times as a child he had baited my hook with a muddy worm or coached me along in some other aspect of the sport, and something in my heart wished this fish for him far more than I ever could have for myself.

As I watched him move among a million late afternoon reflections in the fast-moving water that day, I knew that what I witnessed was something more than a good fisherman catching a uniquely large and beautiful fish. It was the validation of a lifetime of passion. It was the unexpected and unbound movement of something Holy and true.

It was a gift—finding its way to my own heart and to those I love the most.

It was a fish of Grace.

21

Fish of Grace: Our Fish

I love my Virginia mountains. But I must confess I am no where happier than when I am the first person up on a beautiful morning at the beach. It goes something like this: Awaken to the concave call of the long rolling Atlantic waves . . . check time—6:15 . . . roll gently out of bed . . . steal to kitchen . . . make coffee . . . cut piece of yesterday's danish . . . slip out ocean side screen door and wince as the rusty spring reverberates above the hush of the waves . . .

Imagine youngest son going back to sleep in crib upstairs.

Tackle box, sand spike, fishing pole, chair and coffee in hand, descend the worn wooden steps to the sand below . . . remind yourself that there is no amount of money that can buy the feeling of cool morning sand slipping between your toes as your feet sink into its luxurious grasp . . . lean forward . . . press toward the waves . . . select the perfect spot . . .

Sand spike driven into sand—Pole in spike—Chair unfolded—Coffee to chair—Shirt off—Coffee back to top of tackle box. Let's see . . . oh, damn, back to house for bait cooler . . .

Return with semi- frozen shrimp . . . bait hook . . . time the incoming waves, and measuring the three-ounce weight and tackle behind you, heartily heave the whole thing out to sea. If you've timed everything just right, it will disappear into the water right where the edge of the sun has just begun to rise.

Like I said, it's a glorious thing.

Such was the nature of the morning several years ago as I went through my routine and crept quietly out to the beach. The fishing had slowed down over the last couple of days, but since good fishermen never go fishing for the fish anyway, I heaved the rigging out over the waves and eased down into my low canvas beach chair. The sun's first rays searched a thin line of clouds over the water. A flight of Pelicans angled by on the breeze. Life was exceedingly good.

It wasn't long before the screen door slammed and I was joined by my two oldest children. George and Gussie, (5 and 4 at the time), share the same passion for the beach as their Mom and Dad, but they weren't quite so understanding about the lack of fish—probably assuming (sometimes correctly) that this was somehow Dad's fault. The lack of execution was clearly on George's mind as he greeted me this morning with an exasperated, "Still no fish?"

I tried to explain that often in the case of fishing there is a noticeable lack thereof, but they would have none of it. "We'll catch some today, Dad . . . I just know it," said Gussie.

I slathered them with #30 sunscreen and sent them closer to the surf to work on the day's first castle. I hadn't said anything because I didn't want to shake their optimism, but conditions weren't likely to improve anytime soon—the ocean remained calm and unchanged, as it had been for days, and the tide was beginning to ebb.

I took in the increasing warmth of the sun and watched the children begin to dig by the water. The muddy drips of wet sand fell sloppily through their little fingers. It had been such a wonderful week. I felt incredibly thankful, for both them and these moments to share.

It was then that I had the sudden inkling to pray for a fish.

I am not one given to prayer for such things. In fact, I am

Fish of Grace: Our Fish

not one generally given to prayer outside of the "usual times" at all. But every now and then it seems I am given the whisper. Which is one of the truly remarkable things about praying—to do it right, somehow requires the help of the one to whom you're praying.

In this case I had felt a nudge, so with what must have been the guidance of the Holy Spirit, I offered it simple and sweet, "If it be in accordance with your will Lord and it suits the purpose of the day—send a fish for these children . . . ," I hesitated, "and make it one we can eat . . . Amen."

That last line was really bold of me. We generally caught plenty of fish at the beach, but rarely were they of an edible size or variety. But what the heck, if I was going to ask the maker of the universe and all that was good for a fish, I might as well ask for the whole enchilada.

I opened my eyes and glanced at the tip of the rod. Not more than three seconds passed.

"Bip . . . bip . . . bip, bip . . . ," the rod tip twitched, and then "ZESSSSSS . . . ZESSSSSSSSSSSSS!"

We had a fish.

"FISH ON!" I yelled, loud enough for people to hear a quarter mile away. George and Gussie came flying up the beach wide-eyed and full of wonder.

"What is it?!, What is it?!" they asked in excitement.

"A fish!" I responded.

"But what kind?" one of them queried.

"I don't know," I replied. "It's still out there!" I pointed out over the ocean towards France.

"Gosh, Dad . . . how did you catch it?" George asked, as Gussie began to take her turn at the reel.

"Well, what do you mean, how did I catch it," I began to respond, "I put the bait on the hook and I . . . ," I hesitated a moment.

I had almost already forgotten.

"... and I prayed."

Whispering Loud and Clear

"And you prayed?"

"Yup . . . , I prayed."

"Wow," George said.

"Wow, is right," I replied.

When George finished his tour of duty on the reel, we had one of the finest twenty-one inch "Taylor Blues" I have ever seen.

Gussie looked up with a beaming smile and said, "I knew you could do it, Dad."

"Uh . . . I think God might have caught this one for us Gus." I really was at a loss for words. Blue Fish such as the one we caught normally swim in large schools and there wasn't a sign of activity up or down the coast.

Just a coincidence? Maybe so, but if you want my thoughts on where that goes read, "Just A Coincidence" on page whatever it is . . .

Coincidence or not, I'll tell you one thing—walking up to that cottage with that fish and the children dancing around me drunk with glee was one of the genuinely happiest moments of my life. We immediately cleaned our beautiful prize, covered it in butter and broiled it in the old cottage stove. Would you believe me if I told you it was the best tasting fish I've ever had?

But I have not prayed for a fish since. I guess I'm saving it for another "dry well" moment. Or maybe I'm just afraid I won't get the same result. But perhaps it is because I know now more than ever, that not even prayer is needed for most "fish of Grace." Generally they just come, asked for or not and never given on merit.

Such is fishing, I suppose—and such is the Grace that is given in the everyday of our lives, from an unimaginably loving and joyful God.

But if you happen to have the urge . . . I recommend you pray.

And don't be afraid to ask for the works.

22

Fish of Grace: Broaddy's Fish

It had been a very difficult time. My friend Broaddus Fitzpatrick had just lost his father, Judge Beverly Fitzpatrick, to cancer and though much of the grieving had begun at the time of his diagnosis many months before, there was still a long, long way to go.

The Judge was—is a remarkable man. I can say that because I imagine his legacy will be carried on long after most of us have departed this world. He was part judicial entrepreneur, part mechanical engineer, part spontaneous comedian and always a dedicated father and restorer of lives. He was a friend to everyone he met, and if he had any enemies (though I suspect he didn't) I imagine they would have told you, that in spite of the issue between them, he was still a pretty darn good guy.

Judge Fitzpatrick passed away on Saturday, September 16 while my family and I were out of town. When I arrived at the funeral home late Sunday night there was still a long line of people that extended out of the Chapel and halfway down the block. They had been coming for over four hours and there was no indication of it letting up anytime soon. The Judge had touched more lives than even the family had known.

Whispering Loud and Clear

When I finally reached the front of the line an hour later there were still several people behind me, and there was little time to speak. We exchanged hugs, and typical of the Fitzpatrick family there was a feeling from all of them that the hug was given more than it was received—a hug of assurance and thanks to those who had come. I was grateful for both.

As I was leaving, Broaddus leaned over and whispered in my ear, "Let's go fishing."

"Thursday," I said.

"See ya then," came the reply.

Broaddy had a steady, solid look in his eye. He had been grieving for months, and I suspect he realized he needed a quiet moment away. His passion outside of his family is fishing, and I knew that maybe a day on the water could provide some healing and perspective that might not come as quickly otherwise. I was honored he wanted to go with me.

Unfortunately, the forecast for Thursday didn't look so good—there was an 80 percent chance of showers and thunderstorms and the temperature was supposed to drop. But as we departed that morning for my brother's farm on the Cow Pasture River in Bath County, Virginia, the skies broke clear and warm. There was a sense of promise and comfort in the air. It felt unusually good to be "out."

Broaddy and I stopped in Fincastle at a small country store and provisioned for our day on the river—breakfast biscuits, coffee, snacks, nabs, four light beers, two cokes, two waters, and two of the largest beefsteak tomatoes you have ever seen. We're talking state fair material here. We complimented them with a loaf of white bread and a small jar of Duke's Mayonnaise. Broaddy found the disposable salt and pepper shakers on the back aisle.

We made it to brother Jim's property just after 10:00 A.M., and drove down through the grassy fields to a large stand of trees that ran parallel to the river. The worn path continued beneath the shadowy canopy for another quarter of a mile and then emptied out into an extended meadow about a hundred yards wide. We found the old wooden picnic table by the river and unloaded our gear and supplies.

Broaddy is a fisherman's fisherman. And like all such seasoned vets he has the proper gear to ensure success if it is to be had at all. As usual, when we fished together, he wound up lending me several items, not the least of which were some flies he had hand-tied for the day. Somehow Broaddy had never had the opportunity to fish the Cow Pasture River, but he knew what to bring.

"Try this," he said knowingly. The sincerity in his voice indicated how much he hoped for your success before his own.

The morning sun was now rising high in the sky. We pulled up our big green chest waiters and set off for the river just thirty yards away. When we reached it, Broaddy stopped, hesitated and then turned.

"Thank you," he said, nodding his head with a smile.

"I wouldn't want to be anywhere else," I replied.

He kept the smile and headed up-river.

There was really no need to walk far. The stretch of river we were on was an excellent run that provided a nice variety of habitat—the most attractive of which was a fifty-yard long sluice on the opposite side that ran just below an extended length of rock-outcrop. Broaddy began to test the upper part of the run while I worked the lower end. I was a little surprised after several minutes when neither of us had received a strike, but our late start probably wasn't helping our chances.

Upon completing a thorough search of the upper eddies, Broaddus began to fish his way down the run, expertly flipping his line upstream so the fly wouldn't swing unnaturally towards his position. If there was a fish in there and he was thinking of feeding, Broaddy was going to get him. But several more minutes passed and there was still no activity. We

Whispering Loud and Clear

met on a small gravel flat in about two feet of water.

We began to discuss a strategy that would take us up river and then back to the clearing around lunch time. As we talked, Broaddus made an occasional flip of his wrist—casually casting up the sluice in a manner that took every ounce of concentration when I attempted it. He paused for a moment and let his fly drift to the end of the line. It bobbed unnaturally in the middle of a fast-moving rapid.

"You know . . . ," he began to say, "We could just . . . "

Boom! There was a loud movement of water to the right of me and the clicking screech of fly-line rapidly leaving a reel. Broaddus reacted instantly.

"Whoa!" he exclaimed, as he raised his arm up and back to put tension on the line.

"What in the . . . Did you see that!?" He was completely mystified the fish had hit his line in that spot, and so was I.

"I did!" I replied. "That's about the darndest thing I've ever . . . HOLY COW, LOOK AT THAT THING BROADDY! HE"S HUGE!!" The fish was down-river and much closer to me than Broaddus.

"Yeah, he feels pretty big for sure," Broaddus responded. I walked out deeper and got an even better look at the fish.

"NO, I MEAN HUGE, HUGE," I added. "Stay here I'm going for the camera in the car!"

"Stay here??" came the puzzled response, "Where do you think I'm going?!" I had made it about five steps when Broaddy finally got a good look at the biggest Rainbow Trout either of us has ever seen in a Virginia river. "OH MY GOODNESS . . . RUN!!!" he yelled.

And I did.

When I returned, he had just landed the fish and was taking great care not to hurt the beautiful creature. "Here, take a picture, quick," he said. The fish was so large it looked unnaturally "bull headed" for a trout. I told him that for a moment I thought he had caught a fresh water Dolphin. Broaddus gin-

Fish of Grace: Our Fish

gerly eased the beautiful rainbow back into the water. It hesitated a moment and then instinctively pumped hard for the safety of the deep water along the opposite shore.

All Broaddy could do was smile.

All I could do was smile.

Finally I said, "You know, they don't catch fish up here like that."

"I know," he replied staring back at the spot where the fish had just come from. "I've never caught a fish like that before . . . anywhere."

I couldn't help but comment.

"I think maybe the Judge had something to do with that one Broaddus."

"I was thinking the same thing . . . ," came the reply.

"Third 'fish of Grace,' " I said simply. Broaddus had long since heard me tell of the two others.

"Third 'fish of Grace,' " he said slowly in agreement, his smile widening as the Spirit moved around us.

We had the tomato sandwiches with a cold beer and chips.

God is exceedingly good.

23

Big Bangs and Buckyballs

Damn.
A Comet.
I've just been advised that every 100 million years or so we get slapped by one large enough to produce an "extinction event."

An "extinction event?"

Sounds a little mundane as a description that at the very least would wipe the works of Beethoven from the universe. Armageddon has a much better "going to wipe you out and pound you into smithereens" feel to it. But I guess if our modern English dialect has to describe everything as an "event" of some kind, it will have to do.

The same article that enlightened me to this fact came to the astounding realization that each new species that "takes over" after such an "event" has about 100 million years to grow-up and :

    A. Realize that there are big dirty snowballs "out there" capable of rendering us past tense on any given day.

    B. Come to an agreement that something needs to be done about it.

Whispering Loud and Clear

C. Devise a means by which to avoid the next impact.

I think we have the "A" part down pretty well. Heck, Copernicus probably had some concerns over some of the stuff he saw whizzing by out there. But I'm not certain we've made it to "B" yet. Save some pretty challenging rhetoric by the late Carl Sagan, whose pronunciation of such words as "Nebulae" and "Cosmos" probably didn't help his efforts, we've heard very little regarding our now certain destruction by a wayward ice ball. But it's just a matter of time . . .

How do we know?

"Buckyballs" are how we know.

"Buckyballs??"

Yes. Buckyballs.

Now, I know you're thinking that I'm setting you up for some sort of "Snipe hunt" here, but stay with me a moment. Only recently discovered, Buckyballs are infinitesimally small carbon structures that are hard at work way down there at the sub-atomic level. If you're one of those people that has to "visualize" everything, imagine about seventeen quadrillion jillion little soccer balls all balancing together on the head of a pin that has been shrunken to about one, one millionth its normal size. Now pick one out and separate it from the group.

There—got it? That's a "Buckyball."

Now here's the good part. If I understand them correctly, and I think I do, these science guys have figured out that Comets pulverize our cute little planet every so often because they've taken some of these itty-bitty little soccer balls from certain levels underground and tested the "air" between their "walls" and come to the conclusion that there are traces of stuff that simply cannot be made here in our Solar System. Further, they have determined, by means as yet revealed, that these substances were produced "in some distant primordial environment" which is to say that they came from an oozing and dripping sort of place a very, very long way away.

Now that's what I call science.

Not only have they done something that to the average hard-working, NASCAR watching, blue-jean wearing American must sound like the work of the Gods, they have also been able to infer a conclusion that sounds eternally true, no matter how you slice it.

And it probably is. The existence of "Buckyballs" not withstanding.

So the question remains. What the heck are we going to do about it?

If you saw the movie "Armageddon," which I didn't, let me assure you that no matter how good the special affects were, we are not going to be able to send sixteen oil drillers into space to detonate a large atomic bomb on, in, or near an asteroid or comet anytime soon.

It's just not going to happen.

This makes the 1970's movie "Asteroid," where the Chinese and Russians join us in launching every last ICBM we own toward an oncoming space rock, a whole lot more believable. And if our best hope has ANYTHING to do with 1970's disaster movies we're in some BIG trouble.

The reality of the situation is that "the end" will come. Just as we ourselves are not immortal, it seems likely that our cozy little planet is no less so.

If you're inclined to believe that life on this planet, and the "consciousness" it brings, is merely the result of a little chance and some good luck resulting in a big bang at both the beginning and end, it's not such a pretty picture. Nothing much matters in the end because that's just what it is, and death will finally get its due.

But if you're brave, humble and faithful enough to think otherwise, it's when the real party begins—when all the "what ifs" and "should haves" and injustices of this fleeting world

Whispering Loud and Clear

disappear with the darkness, and the great mystery is understood as we now are understood, though we know not how.

It should be quite a celebration . . . or "celebration event" as the case may be.

Hope to see you there.

24

Fishing for Eternity

I took my two daughters, Gussie (six) and Jane (almost four) back out to my friend Al Hammond's farm last Friday for a little fishing expedition. We arrived at the pond to the realization that the water was still quite muddy from recent rains, but having never truly "fished only for the fish," we shifted our old "Willys" pickup truck into four-wheel-drive and headed down the grassy hill to the water's edge.

After rigging up and sending Gussie over to the dock with a bobber and a worm, I backed the truck close to the waterline and outfitted Jane with the same. She sat on the tailgate to avoid the mud as I flipped the light little rig out over the water.

"Ker-plop," it rippled the perfectly still surface and then bobbed to a stop.

"We're fishing," said Jane.

"Yes we are," I replied as I joined her on the back of the truck.

The day was remarkably beautiful. The temperature was hovering perfectly in the mid seventies, the sky was crystal clear and the grasses and shrubs had just begun to reveal the first lime green hints of their coming Spring glory. It wasn't long before Jane began to fidget, so we broke into the Cokes and Doritos we had on board. I leaned back against the

Whispering Loud and Clear

warm metal panels of the truck bed and sipped the sugary concoction."What a great day to not catch fish," I mused. I began to drift with the high puffy clouds above the tree line. Moments later Gussie proved the thought entirely wrong.

"DAD, I GOT ONE!" she yelled. Her shriek had both elements of excitement and fear.

"Hang on, I'm coming!" I replied, grabbing our little net off the back of the truck.

By the time we arrived at the dock, Gussie had already landed a beautiful rainbow trout—over sixteen inches long and perfect for grilling. Al had advised us to keep a couple to help deplete the stock in the pond before summer, so we wrapped it up in the Doritos bag and put it on the bottom of the cooler. Gussie declared that it was her "lucky bobber" that had done the trick. It was then that Jane started to cry.

"I wis I had a bucky bobber," she pouted.

It hadn't taken long for Jane to reach the point where her own lack of a fish was just more than she could bare. She began to cry harder. Gussie and I needed another fish and we needed it fast, but between Jane's crying and all that muddy water, I figured it was a long shot at best. We re-baited the hooks while Jane continued to sob.

"Come on Gus we'll cast off the dock and see if we can catch another one."

But there was no such luck. Another twenty minutes passed without so much as a nibble. Jane had fortunately quieted down and had even mustered up the moxie to come over to the dock with the can of worms and dirt.

"Maybe I can help," she said quietly.

"YES Jane," I replied enthusiastically, "I bet you can." I handed the rod to Jane and then looked out at the bobbers. The two lines had become entangled. "Reel yours in Gus and we'll see if we can untangle these lines." As Gussie's bobber approached the dock, dragging Jane's in tow, it suddenly submerged.

Fishing for Eternity

"Whoa! I've got something, Dad!"

"What? Are you sure? I think that's just the . . . ," I was wrong. Suddenly, the water right next to us exploded as a huge Rainbow Trout rolled and whipped its tail out of the water. Jane's eyes grew wide with excitement.

"THAT'S MY FISH! THAT'S MY FISH!" she began to yell, all the while stepping backwards lest she come too close to the beast. The fish really was big and a fighter to boot. It was all Gussie could do to hold the little rod in her hand.

"DO SOMETHING, DAD!" she yelled. And I did. Grabbing the little crawdad net that would hardly hold a bluegill, I swept beneath the fish and swung it over the dock. No sooner had I done so, the huge trout wiggled itself out of the tiny net and onto the old wooden planks.

If we were in a slight state of pandemonium before, we were now ready to redefine the word. It may have been Jane's fish out there in the water, but now that it was on board, she was having none of it. Jane was half scrambling, half falling, half crawling to separate herself from the "leviathan" that was frothing there on the dock. Gussie was overwhelmingly enamored with the size of the fish and was screaming at the top of her lungs to "GET THE FISH, DAD! GET THE FISH!!"

The fish had all kinds of fight in it and began flopping and twisting and rolling all over the dock—increasingly wrapping itself in both lines and tugging back and forth with its every movement the free pole that Jane had long since abandoned. This had the effect of swinging the second hook wildly about, and I was now using half of the faculties I had left just to keep it from catching me or the children.

To make matters worse, the dock we were on was only about three feet wide, and between dodging the hook and attempting to grab the fish, I had to make sure that none of us wound up in the drink. I was displaying some pretty good moves, but I wasn't coming up with the fish.

119

Whispering Loud and Clear

Just when things couldn't get any worse, Jane grabbed the can of dirt and worms and began to back off the dock at a high rate of speed, but she tripped and the black mess went down the front of her shirt and onto the dock. This wouldn't have been so bad, but some of the dirt went into her shoes and Jane was convinced that the worms had traveled with it. She began to shriek, at a decibel approaching that of an aircraft engine, "WURMS IN MY SHOES!! WURMS IN MY SHOES!!!"

Having heard this, the fish was no longer the thing for Gus, who promptly dropped her rod and went over to "help" her fallen comrade. By this point the Trout had become a thread bobbin, so wrapped in fishing line as to be mummified, but it was still capable of pulling the conflagration about the dock as it flipped and flopped with abandon. For a moment, I thought the whole teeming mess might go over the side and to the bottom. Forgetting the wayward hook, I pounced upon the eighteen-inch trout and the whole sordid thing came to an end.

It was not a pretty landing.

"Nope, no worms in there," Gus said matter-of-factly as she peered inside one of Jane's shoes. She glanced over at the exhausted Trout. "Say Dad . . . do you think we can keep that one too?"

All I could do was laugh. It didn't take long before the girls caught on to the hilarity of the moment and we all sat laughing there together, snorting like a bunch of little pigs as we recounted our favorite parts of the "scene." Every time we got back to the "Wurms" in Jane's shoes we started howling all over again.

There is a wonderful description in one of Frederick Buechner's books where he recalls a simple morning when he is picking his children up from a bus stop in the country on a clear fall day in Vermont. It occurs to him, at some point during this moment, that no matter what else happens in his life, this world or the universe for all time, that that

Fishing for Eternity

moment is "inviolate". . . . that regardless of how unsafe or uncertain the future may be, that the "having-beeness of this time" is with us forever.

"In all the vast and empty reaches of the universe," Buechner writes, "it can never be otherwise."

For the sake of memories such as these, I hope he's right.

"The Alphabet of Grace"
San Fransisco: Harper & Row, 1985.

25

Attitude is Everything

Tuesday, October 24 must have started out like any other day for Robert Marsteller. He had breakfast with his wife Maralyn and then helped her prepare their two children for school before heading out the door with half a bagel balanced atop his coffee mug. Robert had recently left an investment management position at a leading bank in Washington, D.C., and he was in the process of discussing some new business opportunities with several people who's opinions he valued. The day would be a full one of meetings and interviews.

His morning and lunch meetings had gone well, and as he walked the familiar sidewalks of downtown Washington the bright fall afternoon added to the promise of new possibilities that his recent career change had brought. The day had an unusually clear quality to it, even for autumn, and everything seemed to be exactly as it should be on such a day. Even the man selling pretzels on the corner appeared to be placed there by a director looking for a quintessential scene in a Hollywood movie. Robert's thoughts drifted to his next meeting as he placed one foot in front of the other toward his destination.

He would never make it.

There was a screeching sound of black rubber on concrete

Whispering Loud and Clear

from within a parking garage to his right, and as he turned to see what was happening he was met with the instant and sinking realization that there was no way he could escape the impact of the car now racing towards him. He instinctively jumped as the car neared him to avoid being run over and somehow managed to stretch his arms across the hood as the out-of-control vehicle picked up speed and careened wildly across the street. He clamored to hold on, but the car struck a UPS delivery truck at a violent angle, and he was slung off hard and sharp into its lower left side. The car continued forward, striking several other vehicles before coming to a stop half a block away.

It all had happened so incredibly fast, but also in another sense, so strangely slow. He had never lost consciousness— in fact his mind somehow seemed even clearer than it had been just moments before. He spotted an armored delivery truck across the street and for a moment he thought he had been hit by someone fleeing the scene of a robbery. But the deliberate actions of the men driving the Brinks truck told him otherwise. "We've called 911," they calmly advised him.

"Th-th—thank you," his voice sounded strange and somehow distant. But the sensation of his crumpled body was even more unusual. He realized almost immediately that he didn't feel a thing.

Robert Marsteller was paralyzed from the neck down.

The next several hours were a blur of hospital lights and faces and the rubbery smell of oxygen masks as a Neurotrauma Team worked to restore Robert's C5 vertebrate. They utilized bone stock and titanium to fashion a new one as Robert's had been completely crushed when he struck the UPS truck. It worked well to the degree that it provided stability and structure to the tissue and adjoining bone, but it could never duplicate the original. Without significant progress in medical technology Robert may never walk again. He has regained the use of his arms but has very

Attitude is Everything

limited ability in his hands.

But based on a conversation I had with Robert the other day, his life is far from being over; in fact, the way he sees it he "has a lot to be thankful for." We all do, of course, but perhaps the ironic difference is that by virtue of his accident Robert knows it and "lives it" each and every day.

I asked him about the biggest challenge he has faced since the accident.

It wasn't the numerous operations to repair his spine or the pain and daily grind of physical rehab, nor the countless hours wondering how the immediate needs of his family would be taken care of. It wasn't even the four-week period during which his liver enzymes skyrocketed causing his body temperature to elevate upwards of 104 degrees or even the time he had to be intubated and revived by a trauma team due to a blockage of his airway.

Biggest challenge? Remembering the incredible responsibility HE has for others, and realizing that how he handles his situation can be a "blessing or a burden for everyone who knows him."

"You've got to make the best of what your situation is," he told me. "It's not so much where you end up physically after rehab that is important, as it is where you wind up mentally and spiritually and what you can do for others."

I pondered his words a moment, "You've got to make the best . . . it's not so much where you end up . . . as what you can do for others."

You would be hard-pressed to find better words to live by.

I tried to imagine my own attitude in the face of such a challenge. Would my outlook be so incredibly brave? I thought a moment and then began to compare it to the one I had carried with me that day. If it was any indication, I had some "gauges to reset" before I reached the place that Robert had found. I tucked the lesson away and continued to listen as he told me how important it was to keep his sense of humor about him.

"I've had to remind several people that my accident could have been much worse," he said. "I'm lucky to still have the same amount of brain damage I had before the accident."

He also told me that some of the nurses didn't seem to understand it when he gave them a sarcastic dissertation on "why the Americans With Disabilities Act was the worst piece of legislation ever passed by Congress."

"They need to lighten up a little bit," he said. "Most of them took me seriously!"

I also asked him about the biggest blessing he has realized since the accident. He didn't hesitate.

'The overwhelming support of family and friends," he responded. "I knew I would have friends who would help out, but I had no idea the number, or the extent to which they were prepared to go. Words simply can not describe it . . . it has been so far beyond my imagining. The updates that go out every couple of weeks from the group that put together the website now reach over 800 people."

He was silent for a moment.

"I'm a very lucky guy," he said.

Unlucky perhaps, to be walking in the wrong place at the wrong time as the everyday events of the world conspired against him . . . but the luckiest man you'd ever want to meet when it comes to family and friends who would go to the ends of that same world for him.

And perhaps luckier still to understand so clearly just how "lucky" he is.

Godspeed in your physical recovery Robert. The one you've already made is an inspiration to us all.

26

"The Perfect Flu"

The flu came early to Stanley Avenue this year. It came early and it came hard—and it came without mercy. Like some kind of heathen invading army, it targeted the house on the eve of a major holiday—Thanksgiving—and leapt upon us while we slept. It was a VERY successful attack. I have just reached a point where I think I can write about the whole sordid thing.

First let me clarify the shot issue. My wife and I invested our ten dollars each and received our shots. It was a first time ever flu-shot for me. Shots, as I suspected then and fully know now, do not work. In fact they worsen the Flu severely by reminding you of the money you've wasted at just the moment when such thoughts are hardly tolerable. Somehow they make you feel like you almost PAID to get the stuff—kind of like forking over the $60.00 to go deep sea fishing and spending the whole afternoon bent over the rail. It is not a good feeling.

Someone remarked shortly after this episode that we must have gotten "Beijing Type B" or "Hong Kong A" or some other strain that was not covered by this year's inoculation. I quickly corrected them.

"No, you don't understand. This wasn't some mamby-pamby little oriental thing. This strain was from Morocco or the Sudan or something. Its real name was likely "Pharaoh's

Flu" or "Herod's Revenge" or "Flu of The Great Kahn." It didn't take prisoners and it didn't take names—it took YOU—and rung whatever you thought you were, inside out. Chinese it was not." From descriptions I've read in early National Geographics it was about one step short of Malaria. In fact, given my druthers I'd take my chances with a good ol' jungle fever any day.

It started, as it always does, at "Viral Club." This is a small group activity in which young children get together with the express purpose of wiping their noses, mouths and hands all over everything and each other for several hours. These clubs meet once a week at churches and preschools in the winter months, and are very successful in achieving their primary aim, which is, of course, to infect as many kids with as many viruses as possible. Recently I submitted a suggestion to the Journal of American Medicine that all new strains of flu viruses be named after the church or preschool of origin in lieu of the so-called country. This gives a much more accurate and useful description than is presently available. Examples might be :

Fallon Park Elementary—Class A
Second Presbyterian Preschool—Type 2—Wise Owl Derivative.
Honey Bear Learning Center Sub Strain B
Roanoke City Basic Type 1

We are fairly certain we had "Second Pres. Busy Bee Type 3" as our youngest daughter who attends this particular club was the first to succumb. We also knew we were in some pretty serious trouble, as anything that can sap the energy of this two and a half year old has got to have some serious "oomph." Suffice to say, that within eight hours it had spread to all four corners of the household save one— and unfortunately it was mine.

In a family of six, there is only one thing worse than

"The Perfect Flu"

getting sick, which is, of course, not getting sick while everyone else, INCLUDING MOM, does. I figured I was in for a tough couple of nights, but little did I know we were about to be overtaken by "The Perfect Flu."

There was one moment somewhere along about the third night around 2:00 A.M., as I sat next to my five-year-old in the bathroom offering "commode comfort," when I knew— I mean I KNEW—it could not get worse. I was washing sheets and cleaning carpets and bringing juice and filling vaporizers and wiping "hineys" and making beds and doing all the above with the sort of sleep deprivation that brings madness to Navy Seals in training. It was at about this time, as I sat pondering my predicament, that the dog came around the corner and threw up at my feet. I watched her amble slowly down the hall and curl up under a table. She gave a heavy sigh. I was wrong. It could get worse.

And it did.

Two days later, Sunday morning broke with overcast skies and threatening rain. The weather inside wasn't much better. Mom was still down, and I only had two of the four children semi-back to speed. I had slept perhaps eight hours in five days. Mother Theresa was slowly becoming "Nurse Wratchet."

I shuffled downstairs, put on some coffee and eyeballed the growing pile of dishes in the sink. The counters were a mess of ginger ale stains and saltine wrappers. The trash was piled high around the can. I figured I should at least get that out. I stacked the week's extra refuse on top of the lid and grabbing both sides began my journey to the alley out back. Halfway up the yard the top part of my load shifted and a tepid mix of paper, cans, coffee grounds and fruit rinds cascaded to the ground. I clenched my hands and let out a hard breath of exasperation. Why had I been sentenced to such a perfectly miserable week? Thanksgiving had come and gone and I had been left the role of the sleepless maid—missing almost all opportunities to get together with family and

Whispering Loud and Clear

friends. I let go a second angry groan of frustration and began to pick up the scattered trash.

It was then that I saw it. It was a picture on the front page of the Saturday edition of the Roanoke Times. It had gone unread.

An AP photographer had captured two small children running shoeless through the snow and mud of earthquake-decimated Turkey. They were carrying a small packet of food back to the unheated tent that housed their family. Their faces were bright and alive and they were smiling as though they'd just seen Christmas.

I stood there in my robe and slippers and studied the youthful smiles. As I did, I glanced back at the house where my sick family safely convalesced and then up and down the back yards of our typical suburban neighborhood. I brought my eyes back down to the page. There was thanksgiving and joy in those smiles. There was a spirit of confidence and trust in the midst of overwhelming tragedy that I had failed to muster even in my relatively petty circumstance.

As my two-and-a-half-year-old would say, I felt "a lot a bit" small.

That picture, revealed to me at that particular moment, healed me in much the same way Dickens' ghosts had done for Scrooge. Unawares, I had found myself in need of a good dose of perspective, and when I had failed to garner it on my own, it had been given anyway—clear and concise and right on time. I can see those smiles like it was yesterday, and it is my hope that no amount of temporal difficulty will ever blur their memory. After I collected and dumped all the trash in the big can out back, I straightened the newspaper and placed it flat on top. I guess I was hoping someone else would come along and see it.

Three days later the dreaded "Busy Bee Type 3" caught up with me.

Somehow, it really wasn't that bad.

27

Trust

It is July 1, 1995. My friend, Mark, and I have taken our families to his parent's beach house outside of Charleston S.C. It is Saturday Night and Mark and I are beneath the house in the carport. The girls are tucking the children in bed, and having forgotten a tape deck, we have snuck down to the car to listen to a tape by Dwight Yoakam.

Mark and I are close friends, but lately family and career responsibilities have kept us apart. It doesn't take long before we have turned up the music and begin to sing and laugh and tell "war stories." The conversation winds like a stream from our early days of knowing each other in High School to our firstborn children, both boys born three days apart. Eventually one of the girls calls down the steps and tells us they are going to bed. We say we will be right up. We have lied. We don't come up for hours. It is a great first night at the beach.

But it is not followed up by a very good one. At least not for Mark. He awakes with a fever and headache and other flu-like symptoms. He comes down to speak with us on the beach that morning, but you can see it in his eyes, he does not feel well. A short time later he tells us he must rest and returns to his bedroom. By that afternoon things are much worse, and his wife, Margaret, takes him to a local Medi-Center where he

Whispering Loud and Clear

is diagnosed with "a touch of pneumonia." They give him some over the counter fare and send him home.

But when he arrives he feels worse than ever and goes immediately to bed. I tell him to signal us if he needs anything by dropping a tissue on the floor next to the bed that we can see when we walk between the family room and the kitchen. He has gotten very weak and this way he won't have to yell for us, and we won't have to wake him up to check on him. A couple of hours later I see a tissue lying next to the bed. I walk in and lean over Mark who is facing the wall on his side. "You O.K., Pal?" I ask.

Mark can barely offer a raspy whisper. "I can't move," he replies.

"What?" I respond.

"I can't move . . . I mean, I can . . . but I can't . . . too weak . . . " He is breathing heavily from trying to talk. I tell him I am going to get Margaret who, aside from being his loving wife, is an Intensive Care Nurse of over eight years. She takes one look at him and says we have to get him to a hospital. I put him over my back and carry him down the steep steps to their car below. Mark insists that I stay with Beth Anne and the kids. Margaret whisks him to Mount Pleasant Hospital, a twenty minute drive to the west.

The report later that night is that he is doing fine. The doctors on duty feel he has developed a solid case of pneumonia, but nothing that "a few days rest won't handle." They admit him and start some basic IV's to ward off dehydration. About 1:00 P.M. the following day Margaret returns briefly from the hospital and her report is even better—she has gotten him to eat some saltines and drink some ginger ale. Although Mark has requested that no one come see him lest "he ruin their vacation," I insist on going back with her. We decide to take two cars, so I will have a way back. Margaret says she'll meet me there. She needs to drop off some movies on the way.

Trust

It takes me a few minutes to navigate the unfamiliar hospital corridors, but I find the room. At first I think I have read the number wrong. There is someone in the room but his breathing is extremely heavy. He is literally gasping for air. I warily peek around the corner and am shocked to see that it is indeed Mark. He is half conscious and his breathing is so labored that I know instantly that this is not how Margaret left him. I call loudly down the hall for a doctor. There is no response; it is July Fourth and the small hospital is operating on a skeleton crew. I go back to Mark. He is worse, and I feel a swell of panic inside me. Stay calm, get help the voice says.

As I am going out the door Mark's parents arrive. They have just cut short a vacation in Florida to come see how he is doing. I feel terrible that I don't have time to explain the situation. "He's going to be O.K.," I halfheartedly say as I move past them towards the door. Thankfully, they are followed almost immediately by Margaret who hears his breathing and goes immediately to work. She gets him on his side and tells him help is on the way. I am all thankful that Margaret is an ICU nurse, but she is six months pregnant with their second child, and seeing her husband in this condition must be taking its toll.

I have reached the nurses' station and actually must plead for the over worked, under-trained nurse on duty to come down the hall. She finally makes it, and just as she does, another nurse arrives from out of nowhere. She smiles and calmly says, "everything is going to be alright." At exactly that moment Mark stops breathing.

"Call a code," says the experienced sounding nurse as she turns to leave the room. "You'll need an airway and a crash cart." The slow nurse from down the hall fumbles her way over the phone dial and finally makes an all-call. "CODE, ROOM 227!" she yells near hysterically. In what seems like only seconds, doctors and nurses arrive from

Whispering Loud and Clear

everywhere. Someone yells for a "crash cart" but the calm nurse has already delivered it and is speaking to me.

"I think you should gather the family and leave the room . . . there is a little waiting area down the hall. Why don't you take them down there for a moment and someone will be right with you."

She turns and walks down the hall. We never see her again.

The young nurse that does show up ten minutes later is tearful and uncertain of what to say. She can tell us nothing—only that it will be longer. At this moment I more believe than not, that Mark is no longer with us. But I, like the others, am hopeful. We all sit around the table in shock, trying to comfort each other and come to grips with what has just happened. Silent prayer is offered amidst tears. We are in a terrifying dream.

Finally, a Doctor arrives. Mark is stabilized but he is not conscious. They are rushing him to the University of South Carolina Medical Center in Charleston. Somehow our worst fears have made the words "stabilized and unconscious" seem like pretty good news, but over the next 24 hours our hope begins to wane. CAT Scans reveal that the virus, if it is that, is causing Marks brain to swell. The Neurosurgeons have drilled a hole in his skull to relieve the pressure. They have flown in "Super Drugs" from around the country. But nothing is working. By the second night the Chief of Neurology at one of the best medical facilities in the country has told Margaret that the outlook is dim. He has begun to prepare her for not only the worst, but for what he clearly expects to take place. I finally convince Margaret to come back to the house that night to try to get some rest. It is a long ride home.

When we arrive, Mark's mother and Beth Anne take over with Margaret, and I join his father on the deck for the only stiff drink I've probably ever really needed. We talk about the difficult moments of the last few days. We talk

Trust

about God. And we pray there together beneath a silent moon and a million lonely stars. It is very late. Ruben turns in to bed, and I find myself wandering down the front steps and then beneath the house to the exact spot where Mark and I sat five nights before listening to the music and laughing over old times. The weight of the week descends upon me and I began to cry at the thought of losing my friend, and what it would mean to Margaret and the children.

Eventually I compose myself and decide it is time to pray—not just a short or urgent prayer but one that somehow might speak more of what I am really feeling inside. I do not remember what I prayed, but like all prayer I imagine it started out as a one-way conversation . . .

"Dear Lord . . . if there is any way . . . Any way that you can save Mark from whatever has a grip on him, please do it now . . . take it away . . . make him whole and complete again . . . comfort Margaret and the rest of his family and restore within them . . . "

It was somewhere in here that the conversation started going both ways.

"Pray for his will and not your own."

The words seem to come from both within and without me as though spoken in a dream, but I am far from asleep. In fact, I feel especially present in the "here and now" of things. Somehow, I don't seem particularly amazed one way or the other, and the next thought I have is that it is indeed some pretty good advice. But when I try to do it—to really pray for God's will even if that means the loss of my friend, I am completely unsuccessful. I keep "falling off" the thought . . .

"How can I possibly pray for that?" I query.

"You're not," comes the response.

"But what if that is what God's will ultimately is?" I reply.

"Then you'll have to trust him with that . . . " There is a long pause as I consider what this means. Then I am interrupted again by the same thought spoken powerfully within my consciousness, "Pray for God's will and not your own."

And with a little help, that's exactly what I did.

Later the next day in front of a dumbfounded Chief of Neurosurgery, Mark began to squeeze Margaret's hand in response to some comments we made. Within hours he was attempting to spell out letters in the air complete with an occasional expletive. Several more Doctors arrived to witness the miracle that in all of their words "Just should not be happening." As the hours passed and Mark's vital signs improved, even the normally stale air of the ICU ward tasted somehow fresh and sweet. Life could begin again.

Mark went on to make a full recovery, though it took several more weeks in the ICU as well as months of physical rehabilitation to reach what he calls "99.2 percent." (The balance he leaves for when he needs a convenient excuse.) The Doctors were never able to give a full answer on what caused the encephalitis or the amazing recovery that occurred. But I have my suspicions.

My prayers? Like the others that were offered by family and friends during that time of crisis, I am convinced God heard them all. And I am thankful beyond words that in all the mystery of time and space and hope and love they were sufficient to help order things in accordance with what seems to me God's perfect will. I am also thankful for a lesson in trust, that is as essential to prayer as it is to life—and even in the end, to death as well.

Thanks be to God for the voice that whispers not only beyond our everyday reckoning in the deepest part of our souls, but also at times so pure and clear and true that to mistake its nature would be to deny the very life it has come to give.

May we be given the ears to hear it, the wisdom to listen, and the courage to share its power.

28

Nothing to Fear But Fear Itself?

I know many of you will find this hard to believe, given my penchant for manly things like rugby and mountain climbing (on TV) but there was once a day when I was well . . . wimpy.

Like real wimpy . . . like pink-belly puppy-dog wimpy. Like so scared of the nighttime shadows in our upstairs hall that if I had forgotten to "make water" before bed, it was held until sunrise. And even then, if I was the first one up, I proceeded with caution. You never knew what might have slipped in behind the shower curtain during the night.

Needless to say, Halloween scared the daylights out of me—living or otherwise. Trick-or-treating alone was out of the question. So as soon as I was freed of the interminable embarrassment of doing so with Mom or Dad, I insisted on going with my two older brothers. But why I chose to cast my lot with these two, I'll never know.

Older brothers are perhaps one's greatest friends—willing to sacrifice their lives and maybe even their reputations, if little brother is in danger from the neighborhood bully. But given the chance to scare nothing short of "the hell" out of him, they will avail themselves of the opportunity without reservation.

On more than one occasion I turned from a doorway to find the long concrete path behind me empty.

"Jim . . . ? , Randy . . . ? C'mon guys, this isn't funny . . . "

Eventually I would tiptoe down the walk to get a better look up the street to see if they had left me completely behind, only to have every last wit I ever had scared out of me as they roared from behind some nearby bush with arms waving high and wild.

"AAAARRRRRGGGGGGGHHHHHHHHHH!!!!"

Candy was scattered for half a block in both directions as I involuntarily flung my bag into the night sky. If a cardiologist had been able to get an EKG at that precise moment, they could have written several new theories on heart rhythms, I'm sure. This, after pronouncing me dead.

But the best trick ever played came late one Halloween night and was undertaken by someone other than my brothers. In fact, it was Randy and I who suffered the consequences of their "treachery"—in hindsight, a brilliant ploy thought up in the "heat of the moment."

We had all come in from our initial foray and scattered our treasure across the living room floor. A quick survey of our loot indicated that brother Jim had clearly established a superior procurement system. I'm not sure if he had started early, or simply managed to pilfer mine after scaring me to the brink of death, but one thing was certain, he had more candy.

"C'mon Stuart," said Randy, "let's make one more sweep down Brentwood Drive. We can catch up with Jim if we hurry." I was unsure. It was getting late and there weren't many other trick-or-treaters still out. I surveyed the floor once again. Greed and envy got the better of me.

"O.K., but let's be quick," I added.

Randy and I dashed out the back door and through our neighbors' backyards to the street behind us. Within minutes we were at the top of the street making our way back home.

Halfway down the block we came to a house where a party appeared to be going on. There were people dancing in the front room to some very loud music. Most of them were singing rather zealously along with the tune :

"UH, LOOWEE, LOOWEEEE—OHH, BABY, WE GOTTA GO NOW . . . YEAH, YEAH, YEAH, YEAH, YEAH, YEAH . . . UH, LOOWEE, LOOWEEEE—OHH BABY . . . !!

The rest of the words were incomprehensible.

They still are.

Randy and I pondered whether we should go down the short steep drive. The music beckoned to our young imaginations—its syncopated rhythm carrying with it the intoxicating promise of unknown joys through the cool air of the October night. The carport was lit up. There were clearly decorations on the door. "Let's go," one of us must have said. We knocked on the side door several times. Finally a young man of college age flung it open.

"Well, lookie here!" he said gleefully. "Trick-or treaters! You boys are out kind of late aren't you?"

"We're trying to catch up with our older brother—he has more candy . . . " (We tried to look as forlorn as possible.)

"Oh," he replied. "Well I wish we could help you. I'd give you the whole bowl if we had any, but it's all gone . . . I'm sorry but you'll just have to . . . " He paused a moment. "Hang on," he said. "Stay right here." He closed the door. After a few moments he returned.

"Boys, I just checked with Big John who owns the house, and Big John says that you guys are the one hundredth trick-or-treaters! Congratulations! You've won the GRAND PRIZE!"

"Wow!" we must have replied.

The door swung open a little further. A large man who certainly looked like he could be "Big John" was silhouetted by a bright kitchen light behind him. In his arms was a very,

Whispering Loud and Clear

very large watermelon.

"Holy Cow! Look at that," Randy beamed in awe. "The Grand Prize!"

"Yes Sir," said Big John, "and it's ALL yours . . . " He leaned over and placed it gently in our outstretched arms. "Congratulations!" He said again with a hearty laugh. The door swung shut. We were overwhelmed by our good fortune.

"Wait 'til Dad sees this!" Randy yelled.

"The Grand Prize!" I added.

We turned to haul our newfound treasure home. But we had one small problem.

We couldn't carry it.

That driveway might as well have been the Matterhorn.

In hindsight, I can now see the young revelers laughing as they watched my brother and I fall all over ourselves in a desperate attempt to get that watermelon up that hill. By the time we got to the top we were covered in juice and the driveway itself was littered with chunks of bright red fruit as well as some of the candy from our bags. It was one of the best examples of determination meeting futility that the world has ever witnessed. Certainly the best those folks had seen in a while.

By the time we got home, my parents were so worried out of love for us, that they were, of course, ready to kill us. Somehow they weren't as excited about the "Grand Prize" as we had thought they would be. Maybe it was because we only had about one third of the original melon—most of which was now nothing more than scuffed-up rind. I remember Dad shaking his head as he hauled the dripping carcass out the back door. We were hustled off to bed, our bags of loot going unsampled until morning.

I no longer fear the goblins, ghosts and ghouls of this world, made-up or otherwise. It's the unexpected circumstances and my inability to grasp them and react appropriately that scare me the most now—which is "the fear itself"

Nothing to Fear But Fear Itself?

that I suppose Mr. Roosevelt was speaking of . . .

The opposite of such fear is an unfailing trust . . . a faith in a God that can work with even the worst moments that our selves and this world has to offer—a faith that brings with it the kind of peace in which true courage is found and debilitating fear is forever lost.

With such faith we can carry any load.

Even those "Grand Prizes" that were really just melons all along.

29

Hymn Singing 101

Singing in Church has always seemed a little strange to me. From the first moment I stood next to my parents looking up as they crooned (I'm putting that nicely, especially for my beloved mother who while being just that, couldn't carry a tune in the proverbial bucket), I realized that what I was hearing was something other than music. It was a hymn.

The experience was overwhelming really. There, in the front of the church were these giant brass tubes from which all manner of foreboding notes would emanate, and after a couple of bars were played, the congregation, including my poor mother, would try to match the octaves that this infernal machine was producing.

From down there low in the pews it didn't sound so much like something having to do with praise and worship, as the cacophony that might result if a variety of train horns were played in a room full of large waterfowl under great duress. If making a "joyful noise before the Lord" was our goal, we were in trouble. We had him on the run to be sure.

But as I grew in my faith (i.e., I was no longer allowed to doodle, but rather required to participate in the singing of the Hymn), I realized that this was simply the way hymns were performed. It didn't matter whether I attended a friend's church or my own, hymn-singing demanded that people who clearly could not sing, make every effort to do so.

And so I did as well. Until one day, while closely monitoring the efforts of my two older brothers, I realized that neither of them were singing at all. They were moving their lips all right, but no more sound was coming from them than the Pinochio puppets in our basement at home. Mom never had a clue. Within a couple of weeks I had perfected my own lip-synching technique as well. "Milly Vanilly" would have been proud.

But somewhere along the way I started singing again, not loud like the people who can really sing sing, but at least audible enough that I could hear myself. I also began to notice that there were a great many others who sang just as I did, and who seemed to be equally happy that the giant air-breathing monster up front was loud enough to drown them out as well. Our sins were plenty in number already—no need adding our less-than-melodious voices to the list.

But then I met one George Charles Anderson—a man of many gifts to be sure, but not a single one of them having anything to do with the offering of what most of us would define as a "joyful noise." This fact was first bourne out when the good Reverend Anderson submitted a tape as part of his application for the position of Senior Minister at Second Presbyterian Church in Roanoke.

When the tape arrived, I found a note on it offering a disclaimer and apology. Apparently the sound-man had forgotten to mute George's microphone during the hymn in one of the services he was submitting, and thus a very up close and personal and exceedingly LOUD recording of his voice had been rendered that "no human ear should ever be required to hear." His note went on to suggest that perhaps the listener would be best served by proceeding directly to the sermon, bypassing the hymn that would be sung before it "because the truth of the matter is that I really cannot sing."

Hymm Singing 101

My fellow search committee member Broaddus Fitzpatrick and I smiled at each other. Neither of us having matured substantially since the third grade, we went directly to the hymn. Sitting back in our chairs we listened as the first strained bars of an as yet recognizable song began to play softly in the background. It was barely audible. Broaddus reached over and turned the volume up to a more appropriate level—"I wouldn't do that if I were . . . " I began to say . . .

"ALL THINGS BRIGHT AND BEAUTIFUL . . . ALL CREATURES GREAT AND SMALL . . . "

Anderson's voice boomed through the house. Broaddus dove for the volume knob and turned it down. We listened a moment longer to see if the reduction in volume would help. It didn't. The dog got up and left the room.

If mom needed a bucket, this guy needed a backhoe.

Broaddus looked at me smiling, "Well, one thing's for sure . . . he's honest."

That he was. We giggled like school girls. "It was brave of him to send it," I said. "I don't care how good the sermon is, I think I'd have left that one in the drawer."

But as it turned out the sermon was extraordinary and so was he, and almost two years and 200 applications later we wound up calling him to Second Church as our Senior Minister.

And a short time later he taught me how to sing.

It was during our first "Presbytery Meeting" at which his "call" was going to be approved by the governing body responsible for such things that we first rose to sing together. It was a full house and three of us (it may have been Fitzpatrick joining Anderson and I) gathered around one hymnal to sing. I remember thinking that if "All Things Bright and Beautiful" had been chosen, I would have had to leave the building. But it was some other fairly common hymn, and as we all began to sing the first line, it was

Whispering Loud and Clear

Anderson who was singing by far the loudest.

Except this time it wasn't that bad. It wasn't that good either, but it wasn't bad. What it was, was real—sung with an unabashed and uncompromising heart that would make the most joyful noise of which it was capable. It was a "damn the torpedoes" sort of good that said "here I am as God made me, and be that what it may, I shall return such praise as I can with what I have been given."

He didn't say that, of course, but that's what his singing said to me.

And I've been singing like I mean it ever since.

I bet you didn't know that, George.

Thanks.

30

Going Up?

I have a love-hate relationship with elevators.

As a child, however, it was all love—indeed, love at first sight. What a magical machine . . . back lit buttons surrounded by big brass panels, sliding doors and chrome. Elevators smelled like new carpet, and the hydraulic sound that hummed and strained deep beneath their mirrored walls gave them a mystery that was all their own.

Important looking men who wore ties were always getting on and off elevators. They went up and came down from important places.

My first memory of an elevator is of one located in a brand-new public library in Greensboro North Carolina. I was perhaps six at the time. Mom had dropped my older brothers and I off for a city-sponsored summer activity, probably a puppet show or some such thing. I don't recall seeing the first puppet that day—or any other adult sanctioned event, but I do remember seeing the inside of that elevator. It was an Otis and it had the classic concave brass buttons that were surrounded by an acrylic ring that lit up when you touched your finger to it.

But there was even more electronic fingertip magic to be had in that facility. My brothers quickly discovered that if you rubbed your feet on the brand-new carpet in the

Whispering Loud and Clear

brand-new elevator of that brand new library, you could reach out and give your sibling the shock of a lifetime. I mean a good one—the kind that often drew a blue spark from the giver's fingertip.

The game was on.

We must have chased each other in and out of that elevator and up and down those three floors for about as many hours. When mom came and picked us up, I guess she assumed we had just come down from the show. I'm sure we were sweaty and giddy and full of static, but what else was new? She was never the wiser . . . until now, of course. Oh the things moms can learn in these columns . . .

Recently, I was able to relive the wonder of those early elevator days by watching my not quite 2-year-old son take his first ride. Rob's face lit up when I pointed his finger to the button on the first floor of the new elevator at the Rescue Mission's new Chapel and dining facility. This was only possible after five minutes of intense negotiation with his brother and two sisters for "button rights." Rob doesn't know it, but he now owes them about Three Zillion Dollars for the opportunity to press the buttons first that day. True to form they all clamored to press the little up arrow immediately after he did. Surely there are elevator engineers out there who account for such usage.

Rob's eyes grew wide, as a little bell sounded from somewhere and the big chrome door slowly retracted, revealing the little room inside. He peered around the corner, and glory of glories, there were more buttons in there. He took three quick steps to the center of the box and then looked up at me with a proud grin as if to say "look what I've done Dad!" His three siblings clamored in after him as Rob jumped forward to the control panel.

I am convinced you could put a two-year-old in the cockpit of a 737 and he would think he knew completely how to fly the thing. Rob confidently pushed every button at

Going Up?

his disposal. Thankfully the fire control switch had been placed just out of his reach by those same wily Otis engineers. The door slowly slid shut, and the elevator began to almost imperceptibly rise. Rob cast a quick glance my way. He was a little concerned. "Was this all OK? Is this supposed to be happening?"

Moments later we bumped to a stop and the door magically slid open, revealing a whole new world to walk into. Rob was rightfully amazed. He stepped out, looked all around and then gave me his "WOW!" look. He wasn't sure what Dad did down here all day, but it was obviously a pretty cool place to be. We took two more rides on the way out.

But as adults, elevators are entirely different animals. In a world of personal freedom and personal space, elevators force us to get close to one another—even strangers. When you push the button on an elevator the game of chance has begun. You never know who might be waiting on the other side of that door. It's "office building roulette" at its best.

Think about it. Every few seconds around the world, random collections of between two and twenty people are being put into small quiet boxes for periods ranging from just a few seconds to several minutes. B.F. Skinner's Psychology Lab produced no finer experiment in human behavior.

And what do we do?

We stare at the numbers of course. Ninety-nine out of one-hundred people who get on elevators immediately look up and watch the numbers go by. No one looks at anybody. Everyone faces forward. People rarely, if ever, speak. Staring at those numbers is a way of fighting the inactivity and the silence that we are so unaccustomed to, especially in the presence of others. It keeps us from having to engage our fellow man.

When I ride an elevator alone, I'm liable to look around the compartment, inspect it for cleanliness or otherwise just

Whispering Loud and Clear

notice its details. I guess it's a holdover from childhood, but the buttons seem to warrant a lot of my attention. How many? Does the fire alarm / emergency stop button look like it might work? Is there a phone? A thirteenth floor? But if someone else steps on board, I have historically been guilty of watching the numbers. All that silence in the presence of others is just too much.

But maybe it shouldn't be.

Lately, I have been striking up a conversation when possible and practical, whether it's in an elevator or some other public place like a checkout line. And the startling result has been that most of the people that stare up at those numbers or at those magazine covers are just as human as I am. When given the opportunity, they're as happy to share a moment of their lives and their selves as a member of my immediate family would be.

And maybe at the end of the day that's just who they are—a member of my greater family that I will only have the opportunity to know for just this moment. Will I speak into the silence between us if the moment permits? Or will I lose myself and the possibilities in the numbers that flash by above—counting off the floors and even the seconds which I have left to give?

I certainly hope it's the former, for the more strangers I discover to be family, the easier it is to offer the smile or the kind word in the right and fitting moment . . . and the easier it is to believe that ultimately we're all traveling upward together.

How about you?

Going Up?

31

Out of the Mouths of Babes . . .

Children are truly amazing.
And adults are such blithering idiots.

One of the worst acts of violence and hate in the history of man has just taken place and the television networks are showing it over and over and over and over from every angle imaginable. And apparently there were some among us perfectly willing to let their young children watch.

If that's not child abuse I don't know what is.

If you consider the imagery that was broadcast—from the initial plane slamming into the south tower to the people plummeting to their deaths, to the images of the towers themselves collapsing, it is probably, pixel for pixel, the most horrific tragedy ever captured on film. So if you have small children as we do, you likely considered the impact it might have upon them.

Our two-year-old son, Rob, is, of course, too young to have any understanding of the event. On several occasions he bounded happily into the room and then turned with a smile and pointed at the TV repeating, "Fire-tuk, Daddy—Fire-tuk . . . " His typically joyful demeanor provided a difficult contrast to the images on the screen and his intense

Whispering Loud and Clear

reverence for firemen seemed ironic in light of the recent heroism. It was as if he alone were the only one to understand their importance all along.

Maybe he was.

Four-year-old, Jane, was much the same in her lack of "worldly" understanding. But she did catch me off-guard the night after the tragedy, when out of the blue at bedtime she said, "Dad, I'm sure sorry about the buildings that fell down and the people inside. But you know . . . ," she continued as though somehow she really knew, "they're going to be all right." I stared back at her unable to speak.

"They are," she said again confidently. "They're going to be just fine . . . "

"Yes, they are . . . ," I stammered, fighting back the tears in my eyes. Out of the mouths of babes . . .

We wanted our two oldest children, George eight and Gussie, almost seven, to see a small part of the coverage so that they would have an idea of what had happened. After all, it is a part of the world they live in, whether we like it or not, and they need to be prepared to not only be able to discuss it with their peers, but to begin to have some notion of the most difficult aspects of reality.

So we let them watch two short segments of the coverage that detailed what had happened. But we were careful not to let what images they did see overwhelm them. Following the advice of a Psychiatrist who is a good friend, we emphasized the fact that this was an isolated incident and that the United States was a very large country. We also reassured them that in the greater scheme of things it did not pose an immediate threat to them or their loved ones.

Perhaps more important, we were careful not to overly exhibit our own emotions. Children tend to interpret the significance of events and the extent to which they should or should not be afraid by how their parents respond. It's amazing the strength you can find when your children depend on it.

Out of the Mouths of Babes...

The images didn't seem to help our daughter Gussie understand things any better than she already did. She accepted the reality of what had happened mostly as a matter of fact and was willing to leave the rest to God or the President or whoever else might handle such things. But she was very affected by a young girl about her age on TV, who was obviously disturbed by what had happened. After watching her on the news Gussie remarked with clear concern, "I hope that girl is going to be alright . . . " It was just like her to be worried about how others might be affected by the tragedy.

George, on the other hand, had many questions. Who would do this? Who could do this? Where do they live? Did they know they were going to kill all those people on the planes? How can a building just fall down like that? Can we rebuild them? Will our guys be able to find them?

Why did God let this happen?

When you sign on to be a parent you know there will be days when you struggle to provide answers, but nothing can prepare you for the questions you eventually wind up fielding. I remember the advice that an English labor and delivery nurse gave us when George was born. "You're going to get lots of advice," she said with her lilting accent, "but in the end there will be plenty of moments when you aren't sure what to do . . . When that happens you need to follow your heart and do what feels right to you." She paused. "Trust it," she said emphatically. It seemed appropriate now.

I told him that these men lived on the other side of the world in a rugged country called Afghanistan and that they lived in tents and caves and that they would be very hard to find. I told him that they didn't like our country because they thought our actions and ideas were to blame for all the problems they had. I told him that we had known that they didn't like us, but that we had no idea they were willing to do something so terrible. I also told him that our government was

Whispering Loud and Clear

working very hard with all the other countries in the world and that these guys would be on the run until they are caught.

I gave him the final logistical answer in his own language. "They're pretty much history," I said.

Regarding God's will, or lack thereof in this case, I wanted to try and explain the concept of free will and love and how we aren't puppets and that God's passive will is sometimes more evident than his active will. I wanted to tell him that while there is evil among us, ultimately we are given the keys to the kingdom, and whether we're willing to use them is pretty much up to us. I wanted to tell him that just as there will be times when I will allow his decisions to lead to things that cause us both great pain and sorrow, God too, tends to allow us to face the circumstances of our collective actions. I wanted to tell him that in this world we see "but dimly . . . "

But I didn't.

"Sometimes all we can do is trust him," I said. "Even when we don't understand or know what the next day will bring."

"Which is pretty much every day," George responded.

Out of the mouths of babes . . .

32

Big Winning Hearts

About this time last year I wrote an article entitled "Big Losing Hearts." It detailed the exploits and misadventures of my son's rag tag soccer team. By sheer default, I had become their coach. "The Rapids," as we were then called, were a motley collection of leftover and left-out kids, who either signed up late for the league or were somehow left off the teams they had expected to be on. We were young and small and inexperienced and in many ways just plain bad.

We did not win a single game.

Nope, not one.

But we had a heck of a good time trying, and in the process, we discovered that there was desire and courage in those young hearts. So late this summer when practice began, hopes were high . . . high that we might win a game.

At least one.

In the spirit of a brand-new start, we renamed the team the "Rail Dogs"—a fun sort of name to yell when you're eight or nine years old (or 40 for that matter) that also honors the tradition of the railroad town we live in. When the big men in their giant locomotives waved as they passed the park in which we played, we knew they were pulling for us.

Whispering Loud and Clear

We were Rail Dogs. We were one of them.

But just like a train, the first practice started rather slowly. Two of our top three players had "graduated" to the next age group and the two boys that replaced them were entry level players that had little experience. One other new player had promise, but my assistant coach, Bryan, and I had our doubts.

By the second or third week of practice, however, many of these doubts were gone. Somewhere over the course of the last year these boys had learned to listen—that or they had been reading some old Vince Lombardi speeches. They began to pay close attention to the things that would enable them to improve their skills.

"Play your position!"

"Follow your shots!"

"Break to the open spot!"

"Cut off the angle!"

"Be the first to the ball"

"Use your wing!"

"Trust your backup!"

They also approached their ball control drills and other developmental exercises with great concentration. Guys that could hardly look up when dribbling the ball last year, began making crisp, clean passes. Others, that once chased the ball in a sort of rugby scrum all over the field, began to hold their positions. Bryan and I began to think that maybe good things were possible.

But just before the first game, I was nervous for the boys. They had learned how to lose gracefully last year, and they knew that the opportunity to compete was the biggest part of the fun, but they were ready to win their first game. You could see it in their eyes.

"Boys," I told them in the pre-game huddle, "there's no telling how good we are at this point, but I do know one thing—no one has worked harder than you guys to get ready

Big Winning Hearts

for this season, and if you go out there and give it everything you've got and remember what you've learned these past four weeks, you'll have a darn good shot at winning your first game . . . "

The boys looked up, silently weighing the validity of what I had told them. "You really think so?" one of them finally asked.

"You betcha," I replied. "Play your positions, and be the first to the ball and you've got a good shot at this thing . . . " The boys looked around at each other as if to say, "Wow, Coach really believes it."

They were ready to play.

We bowed our head for our pre-game prayer which was generally the giving of thanks for the beautiful evening and the opportunity to play the game. We also asked God's blessing over all who would compete on these fields that night and that we might do so safely and free from injury. I was sure that at least a couple of the boys were questioning whether we ought to be asking God's blessing for the opposing team. I remember thinking about that when I was their age . . . "Dear Lord, we don't want them hurt, but how about slowing number seven down just a bit . . . "

But if they were thinking the same, they didn't say anything.

We broke our huddle, and as the starters headed out onto the field a Norfolk Southern coal train came powering around the bend. The engineer gave a short blast of his horn. The boys all waved gleefully. "It might just be a pretty good year," I yelled to Bryan as the locomotives roared by.

"Might be!" he responded, nodding at the train.

As it turns out it was a pretty good sign. We scored two goals in the first five minutes. After going up three to zero, we tried to "call off the dogs" by dropping our offensive players back to defense and moving our fullbacks to the front. After all, we knew better than anyone what it felt like to get

Whispering Loud and Clear

thumped. But the boys still played disciplined and sharp.

We won the first game seven to one.

We won the last one seven to zero.

In between there were nothing but victories.

Vince Lombardi would have been proud.

But Bryan and I were even more proud of how the boys handled themselves. Even when they were jeered by a couple of teams before we played (annihilated) them, the boys never responded. I did not hear one single word of bravado or bragging the entire season. Out of EIGHT year olds! Can you believe that? I suspect without the lessons of the winless season we would not have known how to act during the undefeated one.

Those who are truly successful in life know how to lose as well as win with grace and dignity, and the 2001 Southwest Rail Dogs have proven they know how to do just that.

Way to go Dogs—you're tops!

33

Two Different Lives

The tapestry of humanity is so broad and wide that brief acquaintances rarely stand out against the montage. But I met two people this past year, the memory of whom I suspect will last a lifetime . . . and maybe beyond.

We vacation every summer in Pawleys Island, S.C., and it is here that I met the first individual of note. We had greeted that morning with great anticipation as the agenda for the day included our traditional crabbing exhibition to the other side of the island. As all experienced crabbers know, very little is needed to crab—a piece of string and some fish heads will about do it. Beyond that, all that's needed is a creek side dock on which to lower the skanky fare to ones quarry. Normally we drive up and down the beach road until we find an un-rented or unoccupied house that has such a dock. But this year we had ventured south during a more popular week, and crab pots aplenty were tied to every dock.

"Hmm . . . ," I thought, "This calls for some creative action on Dad's part." Spying a very large home in the middle of the island with no rental sign and what appeared to be an owner's S.C. tagged vehicle in the driveway, I pulled in and turned to face my three little crabbers in back. "Have no fear!" I said, "I shall go inside this lovely home and humbly

Whispering Loud and Clear

ask permission for use of yonder dock!" I was pretty confident a well-placed smile and considerate request for these three little guys would do the trick.

I ascended the steps of what was clearly one of the nicest houses on the Island. As I knocked on the door I could see a woman moving about a kitchen straight out of Southern Living magazine. A man sat in the corner of a well-appointed room that adjoined. "Too bad this place isn't for rent," I thought. The women opened the door. She appeared to be in her sixties.

"Good Morning, Ma'am . . . My name is Stuart Revercomb and my family is down here on vacation from Virginia. I have three children, and we were wondering if we could get permission to use your crab dock for a few minutes . . . I have a baby sitter to help me watch them, and they all have life preservers on."

She looked at me and reciprocated my smile, "Well I don't see why not, just . . . "

She was broken off harshly in mid-sentence by a loud voice. "HELL NO!" it said. Mr. personality emerged from the shadows to the right from behind a bar.

"Uh, . . . Excuse me, but . . . uh, . . . apparently my husbands not . . . not comfortable with the idea . . . " She tried vainly to cover his rudeness.

There was really no need to say more. That answer was clear enough for me. I apologized for having bothered them and began to turn away from the door when the old curmudgeon continued . . . "NO!" he yelled as if I had asked again which I hadn't. "We don't KNOW you . . . ABSO-LUTELY NOT!" The door slammed behind me.

Good heavens, I thought, if we were looking for crabs we had certainly found one, without so much as dropping a line. I wondered what was getting him. He had looked so sour sitting in his chair even before he began his little tirade. Maybe he was just having a really bad day, but somehow it

Two Different Lives

felt otherwise. The scowl he carried looked like one that was worn regularly and I had a feeling his poor wife lived with this attitude on a regular basis.

Here was a guy who clearly had a great deal more material abundance than most of us ever dream of—A large second home, complete with BMW and Suburban in the driveway. The so called "good things in life" sure hadn't brought him the happiness he must have once dreamed of. By all appearances he was already dead. We washed the dust from our feet and found a more hospitable dock two doors down.

It didn't take long before I began to contrast him to the other most memorable individual I encountered last year. He is quite unlike the unfulfilled wealthy man. For starters he is much closer to poor than not—he holds a job busing tables and washing dishes at a local cafeteria. But he does not find his joy in his paycheck—he finds it in making other people, especially children, laugh. He is a young black man who doesn't own much of a car and likely has never dreamed of owning a house such as the man with the second home in S.C.

But he is a very happy person.

The first time I noticed him I was sitting with my large brood just beginning the spectacle that is often dinner out for the six of us, when I heard him cajoling a smile from my two-year-old Jane. He was busing the table behind us.

"Hey cutey—what's your name?!" he asked bent forward in animation, head turned slightly to the side, eyes and lips smiling wide. "My goodness you ARE a sweetheart . . . Just look at those EYES and that HAIR!" Jane, always the ham, blushed in a rare moment of embarrassment.

And YOU, what's your name?" He questioned Gussie, my oldest daughter. "I bet it's a princess kind of name—bet you could feel a pea under a HUNDRED mattresses!" Princess?! Gussie was putty in his hands.

"That's a fine-looking boy over there . . . you like football

Whispering Loud and Clear

boy?" He had noticed Georges T shirt. "You look like a quarterback to me boy—gonna be a good one too I bet . . . Momma, you expecting another one?" My wife was WAY along. "As pretty as these children are you just HAD to have another didn't you!" Ping! Direct hit—my wife was enamored. He grinned at me . . . "Nice family Dad," he whispered as he went by.

His comments were simple enough to be sure and to some, the interruption would have been just that, but to others such moments, when offered from strangers, are to be enjoyed for the light-hearted gift of one's self that they are. Since then, I have noticed him several times talking and smiling with children as he passes them during his duties. He's a simple man, but he is a beautiful reflection of the Joy and Love he's been given.

Over the last thousand years I'd like to think that there have been a whole lot more of us that have turned out like my friend at the cafeteria in lieu of the dour old man who seemed to "have it all." But I suspect the line is likely drawn somewhere down the middle. Perhaps the next thousand will bring to our collective nature a more compassionate and redeeming spirit, but that of course can all only start in our individual hearts.

Are our lives lived out as we dream they can and profess them to be in our better moments? Do we accept the endless Grace that is given us? Or has our salt lost its taste? Each of us makes the choice on a daily basis, regardless of our situations—wealthy or poor . . . young or old . . . in perfect health or somehow not . . .

My prayer is that we shall all choose well.

34

What Do You Expect?

Getting our four children to school on any given morning can be a challenge.

Getting them to church is even harder.

Sundays at our house are generally a raucous free for all—a Ringling Brothers sort of thing that is part bath house, clothes auction, military chow line and rugby scrum all rolled into one. When it is executed properly, it is a thing of beauty, no less wondrous than a German Symphony. When it goes awry, which is far more often the case, it is more akin to a train wreck. One involving multiple trains . . . six to be exact.

So by the time we get there, and deposit the two youngest in "class" (i.e., "Virus Club"), expectations for the other two are pretty high. After all the effort to pull the whole thing off, my wife and I figure that the least George (eight) and Gussie (seven) can do is sit there and listen a few minutes—maybe even understand something of what is going on around them. You know, follow the words to the hymn, bow their heads in quiet reverence as the prayer is being said, clue in occasionally when the minister is speaking . . .

In reality, of course, this is rarely the case. Gussie usually pays attention to the music but otherwise wanders hopelessly with pencil and paper during the rest of the service. Being a male beneath the age of fifty-five, George has an

Whispering Loud and Clear

attention span of about seven seconds. He continuously squirms like a freshly dug worm, often achieving positions that would be the envy of any contortionist.

If I were to ask him what he remembered most about this past Sunday's service he'd say, "I thought it was terrible . . . I was surprised you tipped her that much."

"We went out to eat on Saturday George . . . I was talking about the Church service . . . "

"Oh."

"So?"

"Good," he'd reply. Which loosely translated means, "same old, same old." Just once, I'd like to get an indication that at least something meaningful had crossed their minds.

Where in the world do we get such expectations . . . that our children will somehow get "the big picture"—and in exactly the way that we understand it? Some expectation is surely good in the sense that it helps point the way toward the goal, but you'd think that our own memory of childhood would remind us that much of our spiritual understanding comes later in life, and often in ways we ourselves had never imagined. If God had the same expectations for us that we have for our children we'd be in some serious trouble.

It's a good thing he has the patience of Job.

Our "Christmas expectations" are often equally unrealistic. There are, of course, two "Christmases"—the one that involves the joyful observance of our "secular traditions," and the "real Christmas" that from a Christian perspective, is ultimately the celebration of God's gift of himself to the world. We all have our own expectations of what both should be like, and if yours are like the rest of us they're probably pretty darn high. And why not? The nostalgic memories of our past, combine with our more meaningful hopes and dreams, and all that Madison Avenue marketing, to produce an image that is about as obtainable as the North Pole itself.

Not to mention Bethlehem.

What Do You Expect?

We mix our "Holidays" and "Holy Days" together like the varied ingredients of an old family eggnog recipe, and then expect the miracle of Christmas Peace to somehow emerge just in time to give us nothing less than a nirvanic epiphany. But the result for so many of us is more often a credit card hangover and an empty feeling that somehow we were never really able to "get into" the Christmas Spirit this year—as if it were something we could pull over our heads like a sweater from our favorite mail-order catalogue.

Christmas for many of us just never seems to quite live up to its billing. Perhaps, it's the Marquee letters that we so painstakingly arrange ourselves that keep it from happening.

A couple of weeks ago, I sat frustrated in the church pew as I watched daughter Gussie scribbling away on the back of a donation envelope. Meanwhile up in the chancel, a choir was performing with a three-piece brass ensemble one of the most glorious pieces of music that our extraordinarily gifted music director has ever presented. Gussie didn't seem to be hearing a note of it, but was intent on eking out each individual letter of whatever she was writing in her seven-year-old scrawl.

When the music finally came to an end, I leaned over and gave her my parental best, "Gussie, you really should listen to the music when they're playing like that . . . did you hear the French Horn and the soloist or were you too busy drawing on that paper?"

"No. I wasn't listening," she confided without hesitation. Her blatant honesty irritated me.

"What was so important that you weren't listening?" I responded. The irritation in my voice was not lost in my whisper.

"A note to Virginia . . . ," she responded somewhat sheepishly. "She wasn't feeling well this morning, and I thought it might make her feel better . . . "

"Oh . . . " I replied, my voice trailing off at the realization

Whispering Loud and Clear

that at least her motivations were good. "Can I see the note?" I asked.

"Sure," said Gus, handing it over. I unfolded it and reoriented it several times until I could make out the childish letters scratched faintly above and below the crease in the envelope.

"YOUR GOD LOVES YOU," it said.

I pondered the words a moment and then turned back to Gussie.

"You wrote this for Virginia?" I asked.

"Yes . . . ," she replied again. "I thought it would make her feel better . . . " I finished the last three words of the sentence with her in unison, nodding my head as I pondered my short-sighted nature. Instead of enjoying the music and trusting Gussie to work out her "end of things," my own preconceptions and expectations had banged and elbowed their way onto the stage once again.

"Trust," said the voice, "and leave it to me."

So far this season, I have managed to do just that. And the joy that is part of the Spirit of Christmas, "real" and otherwise, has found me early and often and ready when asked to play my part in things. It has helped me understand that perhaps the greatest gift that the babe in the manger brings is the knowledge that all those details we concern ourselves with don't really count for much in the end.

So this Christmas, do all those "important" things if you feel you really have to, but don't think for a moment that the music isn't going to play without them . . . for nothing in all the heavens and in all the earth and in all of eternity can stop the multitude of Angels from singing the good news of Christ's birth. The only real question is whether we'll be able to hear it.

"Your God Loves You" said the note—says the music— says the infant in the hay.

Indeed he does.

166

35

True Patriotism

It's hard not to get swept away in the high tide of American patriotism these days—Old Glory is flying higher and higher almost everywhere you go. Even on the open road, we are awash in America's rekindled sense of self and purpose. From pickup trucks with full sized flags whipping urgently in the wind behind them, to the small red, white and blue ribbons atop our antennas, people want each other to know that we're all in it together.

It's a good thing isn't it.

If you haven't gotten misty eyed at the sound of our National Anthem or "America The Beautiful" in the last three months, you are either from another planet or have joined the ranks of the walking dead of this world. Having traveled to Charlottesville for the last three Virginia home football games, I can tell you that when those young men and women raise that flag in the middle of the field and that lone voice is joined by 40,000 others, there aren't many tear ducts lying idle. If there are, it's either a guy on his first date trying to look woefully more manly than necessary, or a young lady who likewise is fighting off the dreaded mascara run.

There is something very special about standing among such a diverse group of Americans—Doctors and Truck Drivers, Linemen and Lawyers, Shop Workers and

Whispering Loud and Clear

Secretaries—and, if but for a moment at least, accepting the realization that we're all pretty much the same beneath the titles and the clothes and the different hues of skin we take so seriously.

Even during the Virginia Tech game there was a moment when I almost felt as one with my Hokie brethren across the way. It was a brief respite from the antagonisms of an otherwise joyful rivalry that ended quickly when they shellacked our quarterback. But for a moment there, I was sure I knew what true patriotism is all about. I recall thinking that if Osama Bin Laden can unite a bunch of Wahoos and Hokies, he's in some serious trouble—which is perhaps best evidenced by the fact that he has the United States Marine Expeditionary Force after him.

These are not people you want on your trail.

All those plans sounded a little better sitting around the campfire, didn't they Osama?

But as powerful as singing the National Anthem among so many fellow Americans has been, it paled in comparison to a recent trip I took with my daughter Gussie's First Grade class to the Veteran's Administration Hospital in Salem, Virginia. A couple of weeks earlier the class had performed an inspiring collection of readings and patriotic songs for the parents, one of whom was so impressed with the performance (we all were of course) that they felt taking the show on the road to the "V-A" might be a good idea. Daughter Gussie had a speaking part and I had never been to the V-A before, so I volunteered to be one of the chaperones.

We all met the bus at 10:30 A.M. in front of the school, and twenty minutes and 78,000 decibels later we arrived at the V-A Center. If your job has been getting you down lately, and you think no one has it quite as tough as you, then I suggest you take a short ride on a school bus full of first graders and imagine yourself as the driver. Given my choice between this position and becoming a member of

True Patriotism

the Marine Expeditionary Force, I'm not so sure I wouldn't take the latter.

But armed with clear and concise instructions from their teachers, the children filed off the bus quietly and orderly and proceeded to the large glass atrium that is part of the main entrance to the 210 Acre facility. They were divided into thirds by their shirts which were either red, white or blue and were quite the sight as they climbed the risers in preparation to sing. A small group of both veterans and care-givers began to assemble, and by the time they had finished their first song, an upbeat rendition of "The Pledge of Allegiance," a nice little crowd was on hand. Gussie recited her part perfectly, which, of course, reflected the extraordinary charm and character of her parents (i.e., she paused in all the right places). The rest of the children did likewise. As before, it was quite the show.

But the highlight for me came as I watched an elderly veteran in a wheelchair, who had lost a leg presumably for the rest of us, come wheeling towards the crowd. He wore a slight scowl and it was clear he simply wanted to cross over to the other side of the assembly to get where he was going. But to do so he had to pass between the children and the audience. He hesitated a moment and then began to push his way across. The introduction to Lee Greenwood's "God Bless The USA" was playing and the children had just begun to sing as he started. About halfway across, they began the refrain:

> *And I'm proud to be an American where at least I know I'm free.*
> *And I won't forget the men who died, who gave that right to me.*
> *And I'd gladly stand up next to you and defend her still today.*
> *'Cause there ain't no doubt I love this land, God bless the U.S.A.*

Whispering Loud and Clear

The grizzled old Vet brought himself to a stop and then slowly turned to behold the children, the stump of his leg clearly catching some of them off-guard. But they kept singing loudly and boldly, and for one brief and shining moment, the sacrifices of his past met the thankful and unbridled confidence of their future, and something of glory was made. He sat there as they completed the song and then as the loud and long applause filled the hall he slowly turned and continued on his way, his tear-stained cheeks matching the vast majority of ours.

I couldn't help but think that those children and that old gentlemen had just given each other something exceedingly precious, and that they in turn had shared whatever had been between them with us. Perhaps it was what amounts to "true patriotism"—the thankful caring and sharing of the trials and joys of one another in the common brotherhood of humanity. A compassion born of something greater than ourselves that realizes that none of us can rest comfortably in our own skins until the rest of us have the opportunity to do the same.

Such patriotism doesn't stop at any particular border, but rather extends to wherever the dignity of human life is valued and prayers of hope for one another are made. It can stretch from the innocent heart of a child to the doubting soul of an old soldier, and even to me and you if we are brave enough to let it.

May God continue to bless America and all "True Patriots" everywhere.

36

All in Time . . .

A friend told me last week that she had had a busy week, "but that it had made time fly . . . " She then asked, "is that a good thing, though?"

Good question. I suppose the answer has something to do with how much you happen to be enjoying what you're doing. Being busy can make time fly. Being busy at something that brings you joy can make it stand still, until you reach a point at which you realize time has been passing and you wish you had more of it.

I have a friend named Tim who knows how to have a "good time." Tim is rather on the laid back side of things. One of those people whom my father must have been referring to when he would say, "if he were any more laid back he'd be asleep." Tim wisely never grew up in many ways—at least in the sense that he felt like he had to buckle down and start a "professional career." He was smart enough to know he was happiest when creating things, and so he has spent the majority of his years as a journeyman artist, photographer and musician. Tim's bands, in their many varied forms, have played around the state since I was in high school, and he continues to do so when "time and weather permit."

When asked why he took such long breaks between music sets at fraternity parties in college, Tim would reply with a very large grin, "Hey, not to worry gentlemen—we're on 'Tim Time' . . . " It always brought a good laugh, even from the "gentlemen" who were ready to kill him for putting such long pauses in the middle of their party. But there was something about the notion of being on some other system of time, beyond that of this world, that I always liked. I got the feeling that if everyone were on "Tim Time" the world might be a better place. Because "Tim Time" was most definitely about letting things pass at their own pace.

Maybe he didn't know it, but I think Tim was pretty close to being on "God's Time."

A couple of years ago I was invited to join a long-standing fishing trip made up of a group of Doctors and their sons that have been traveling to Cape Hatteras since the 1950's. The present day group is not the original of course, but rather a gathering of "honorees" that have received the mantle since the first group assembled so very long ago. Being an event of such "heritage" there are many traditions: a shot of sherry with breakfast, sardines with mustard and hot sauce on the beach, Brunswick Stew for lunch (the rookie cleans the pot in the surf), the smoking of cigars that don't have labels, (imported from some country to the south) . . . the list goes on and on. I'll leave the rest up to your imagination, comfortable in the fact that as creative as it may be, you will likely still fall short of the reality of the enterprise, that at the end of the day, has less to do with fishing than it does "just getting out in it."

But as "unserious" as it may be when it comes to fishing, it's not entirely—for like anyone who pursues such quarry, these fishermen, myself included, like to catch fish from time to time. Nay, most of the time, for if you're going to be "out in it" having a big old time, you might as well be catching fish in the process. So little did I know, as I caught the first fish of the day some three years ago on my rookie trip, that I would be starting a tradition that was likely to be

All in Time...

the source of great consternation if not complete frustration for my newfound fishing buddies.

The tradition?

I would catch all the fish.

I mean ALL the fish. The first trip I caught a Pin Fish, a Bluefish and a two-foot three-inch Red Drum. It was the biggest fish I have ever caught. Total catch by seven other fisherman using perhaps twelve other poles over a three-day period?

Zero. Zilch. Kapatska.

On the second trip I caught a Flounder, seven Bluefish and a two-foot nine-inch Red Drum that was even prettier than the one the year before. I brought him in by the light of the moon on one of the most beautiful fall evenings I have experienced anywhere. I swear I could see that fish in the moonlight for over a minute as he made his way back out through the waves. He seemed to have the glow of another world about him.

Outside of a quick run of bluefish that provided some great angling pleasure for a few of us, everyone else came up with another goose egg. I knew deep down they were happy for me, but I was sure I noticed a sideways glance or two come down the beach the next day. I was amazed they didn't make me clean the pot again.

So this year, when the younger members of our tribe took several of our children down for an intermediate Spring trip, I was certain our luck would change and things would even out. The first day the weather was foul with a twenty-five-knot wind blowing out of the Northeast. The likelihood of anyone catching a fish was extremely low. We had over twelve rods in the water and I figured the odds of something hitting my pole in particular were about as good as winning the lottery.

I should have played it.

I was reaching for a hard-boiled egg when it hit. My

Whispering Loud and Clear

friend Brad was the first to yell, "STU—YOUR ROD!!!"

It had slammed down hard into the sand as a huge Red Drum took the bait and ran. I sprinted up the beach, and grabbing the pole before it disappeared into the surf, wrangled and wrestled the fish to shore. He was two inches short of three feet . . . six inches too big to keep according to N.C. State Law. Whoever heard of a fish too BIG to keep? It was fine with me, however. The children were enamored and had a chance to touch and behold the beautiful creature. We let him go as they danced around the beach in excitement.

My friend, Mark, jokingly yelled, "CUT IT OUT WILL YA!"

"It only happens when I fish with you," I replied.

"It's a good thing the older guys aren't here," he laughed.

The rest of the trip went as usual. Aside from a few small Sand Sharks and "Puffers," mine was pretty much it. That night, Mark's brother, Eric, posed the question, "So why do you think you caught that fish and all the others? Your timing is impeccable . . . how in the world do you do it?"

"I have absolutely no idea," I replied. Then I remembered a moment that morning as we left the hotel—the last ones out. It was our first day, and I was in a rush to catch up with the others who had already been fishing the day before. We had several things to do, including getting the air pressure right in our tires for driving on the beach and picking up some fresh bait. We had yet to rig our lines as well.

As I began to shift into the worldly mode of doing everything in the time I felt we had to do it, I caught myself. Somehow I managed to take a deep breath and relax. I turned to the children and said, "You know, it's during moments like these you have to slow down and relax and take things as they come, and not be anxious about everything you have to do, If you don't, you take yourself out of the world of possibilities that God has for you, and you

All in Time...

create a moment in which it's difficult for the Spirit to work." They actually seemed to be listening. "If we catch a fish today, maybe it will be because we didn't get caught up in forcing the issue right now and are right where we are supposed to be later on—instead of some place we put ourselves by not accepting the flow of things . . . "

I said that, or something close to it. I really did.

I'm not sure they understood every word . . . I'm not sure I do, but we did catch that fish.

Must have been on "Tim Time."

37

How "Successful" Are You?

Quick. What is the first thing you think of when you hear that someone is "successful?"

I still picture some young dude in a freshly-pressed suit, driving a shiny convertible having made lots of money in some business endeavor. It's my "old definition," formed sometime in my impressionable teens, and some version of it still pops up on my mental picture screen until the type of success is defined a bit further. I suppose it's part of the collective consciousness of a competitive and capitalistic American society as well. Talk "success" and most of us jump first to monetary and material considerations.

It is a telling definition and one that speaks more about us than we might care to admit.

Don't get me wrong. There is nothing wrong with success itself in this sense. To the contrary, honest hard work that produces financial success is what enables our society to provide a standard of living for most of its members far beyond any other in human history. There is a strong message to "live and grow and prosper" within both the Old and New Testaments, and Christ's own parables rebuked those that did not invest wisely their "talents" and "salaries." The "protestant work ethic" is just that, ethic, and we lean on it

Whispering Loud and Clear

heavily in our expectations of one another as Americans. But it would seem our relentless emphasis on the defining of success along financial lines has led us to a world that is far less caring and compassionate that it could be, and if you believe in the divinity of scripture, it should be.

Somewhere there's a balance, but it is rare that most of us find it.

Consider pro athletes and entertainment stars, who are certainly the most well-compensated of our society—the most "successful" among us. Typically, they fulfill every aspect of my youthful definition of "success," but so many are rarely happy people in any long term sense. The sacrifices necessary to achieve and maintain such careers are often made at the expense of original family and friends, resulting in a litany of divorces and wrecked relationships. The daily headlines testify to the worst cases. In reaching for ever more career success and material wealth, a large portion of the "ultra successful" find themselves spiraling out of control in a self-indulgent lifestyle that leads to a desperate and often cataclysmic end.

Yet we continue our unhealthy obsession with them, raising their hollow images high above us as we ourselves diligently pursue our own smaller, yet life-consuming carrots. In the meantime the greater beauty of our lives passes by on the side of the road as the worn-out wheels on our heavy-laden carts roll on.

It sure seems like we would be better at recognizing our own potential for true happiness.

But there are those among us that are able to keep their perspective, who do not define their own success in accordance with such a worldly view, and it is they who stand out so bright and real among the lost "successes" of our society.

One such person is actor Ralph Fiennes.

In 1996 Fiennes received an Oscar for his role as Amon Goeth, the ruthless and vile SS Commandant in "Schindler's

How "Successful" Are You?

List," who's emotionless and maniacal lifestyle of sedition and wanton murder make him one of the most heinous villains ever portrayed on the screen. Shortly after making the film, Fiennes gave an interview in which he ironically provides an extraordinary definition of success and what it truly means to be an authentic Human Being.

Fiennes was asked, "hasn't fame and success isolated you from what you were before and those you loved?"

"Success?" Fiennes gave the interviewer a withering look. "Well, I don't know quite what you mean by success? Material success? Worldly success? Personal, emotional success? The people I consider successful, are so because of how they handle their responsibilities to other people, how they approach the future . . . people who have a full sense of the value of their life and what they want to do with it. I call people "successful," not because they have money or their business is doing well, but because as human beings, they have a fully developed sense of being alive and engaged in a lifetime task of collaboration with other human beings— their mothers and fathers, their family, their friends, their loved ones, the friends who are dying, the friends who are being born . . . "

"Success?" he repeated emphatically. "Don't you know it is all about being able to extend love to people? Really. Not in a big capital-letter sense, but in the everyday. Little by little, task by task, gesture by gesture, word by word."

If every one of us believed in such a definition, so that we truly lived it in the "everyday" of our lives, "our world" and "the world" might be a very different place indeed.

How successful are you?

38

Skating on Grace

Watch out my children, the world is an infinitely beautiful and terrible place, full of wonder and grace and unimaginable possibilities that make the heart flutter and the spirit fly. And yet cold and hard and full of sin's dark brooding—where lives and innocence are slaughtered in the cruel and vicious act. But in the end there is . . .

But in the end . . .

The morning paper did what it so often does, wrenching me from one extreme to the other as I scanned the headlines before me. On one side of the page was the glorious picture of Sarah Hughes waving to the crowd on her way to the Gold Medal podium. On the other was the debilitating account of the death of Daniel Pearl, the Wall Street Journal Reporter kidnaped in Pakistan. It was a carnival ride of emotion—on the one hand the intoxicating joy of a young girls unexpected triumph, but on the other the grisly horror of a senseless and brutal murder.

Life made anything but sense.

My wife and I stayed up late to watch the women's figure skating finals. We had packed the four children off to bed, already an hour past their bedtime, with the promise that we would videotape the remaining skaters which were the favorites in the competition. Among them were Michele

Whispering Loud and Clear

Kwan, Sarah Hughes, Sasha Cohen and Irina Slutskaya. Son George wasn't too concerned about the tape—"it wasn't like this was Monday Night Football or anything." But the girls were hooked big time, and they reluctantly made their way up the steps only after repeated promises that they could watch it first thing in the morning.

Sarah Hughes had become my favorite. What a remarkable story she is. The fourth of six children from a blue collar family, Sarah often had to wrangle with her siblings for ice time on the homemade "half hockey rink" her father had put together in their backyard. In lieu of private lessons and tutors and all the other "necessities" so many others use to reach the pinnacle of this sport, sixteen-year-old Sarah still attends her local High School and travels almost two hours by car every afternoon to practice on an ice rink in Hackensack, NJ. She has been doing her homework in the backseat since the sixth grade. She is unassuming and friendly and full of an innocent joy that is as genuine as it is captivating. You get the feeling that Sarah Hughes is exactly who she was meant to be.

But Hughes had finished fourth in the "Short Program," which meant the odds of her medaling were slim. Favorite Michele Kwan was at the top of the leader board, and the whole world seemed to be pulling for her, including my wife. But I had my heart set on Hughes. "Why aren't you pulling for Michele Kwan?" she asked before the final program.

The answer for me was easy. Over the last six months, Kwan had dumped both her choreographer and coach and had decided to go it alone. While this is certainly an athlete's prerogative, I couldn't help but think that these individuals had been "pursuing a dream as well." Kwan seemed cold in letting them go with the simple reason that, "I need to make decisions on my own now . . . " Additionally, she had responded to all of the pre-Olympic press coverage she had received with the modesty of Genghis Kwan—excuse me, Khan—by stand-

182

ing in silent agreement whenever the announcers or inter-viewers heaped praise upon her. It appeared that Michelle was starting to believe everything that was being said about her—not a good idea when you have a competition with the world's best skaters ahead of you.

On the one hand, there was Hughes, full of youthful optimism and sweet humility and a desire to win a medal for her family, friends and country. And on the other, there was Kwan who seemed to be wrestling with a demon that she felt was keeping her away from HER medal. One was now seen as having no hope for the Gold, while the other had all but hoisted it upon her neck. One was daring and creative and willing to lay it all on the line—not skating so much for the results as for the performance itself. The other was simply skating not to lose.

The rest, as they say, is history. Her early fourth place standing allowed Hughes to come out free from her own expectations and anyone else's, and skate the performance of her life (All sixteen years of it). She was loose and smooth and trusting, and with her "self" out of the way, there was room for the Spirit to work, creating an extraordi-narily magical moment—filled with mystery and wonder and something of the divine.

Sarah Hughes wasn't skating on ice. She was skating on Grace.

We watched the tape of the finals with the girls the next morning. They too, were caught up in the magic and joy of the moment as Hughes' dream unfolded like the quintessential fairytale found in all young girls' hearts. Watching their expressions of awe and joy added to the sense of wonderment we already felt. Sometimes things are almost too perfect.

And as I found out a couple of minutes later when the newspaper banged its way to a landing against our front door, sometimes they're just too sad.

The article on Daniel Pearl sent me reeling. He was forty

Whispering Loud and Clear

years old. His wife was seven months pregnant with their first child. He had been a damn good reporter, and by all accounts a fine and loving and giving man. His throat had been slit while someone stood before him with a video camera in hand. What sort of heart could film such a thing? The cold-blooded killing of even your worst enemy? Much less an innocent that had been taken under the pretext of a journalistic interview.

The soul collapses weary and silent under the burden of such news.

What are we to make of a world where such extremes of beauty and pain go hand in hand in the course of our everyday lives? What are we to tell our children? What are we to tell each other? When faced with such headlines, it's hard not to linger on the tragic—to dwell among the horrific words and images they conjure until we have been beaten down to a lesser existence than we would be living otherwise.

But if we can find the strength to believe that our Creator has it all well in hand, in even the worst and most difficult of situations—if we can find the courage to trust him with the "results" that our "performances" might be all they have been created to be—then the quick and fleeting moment that is our life, can be transformed into something "magical" as well . . . , full of mystery and wonder and something of the divine . . .

Get yourself out of the way and trust him completely.

It's the only way to skate on Grace.

39

The Best and Worst of Baseball

I've never been much of a baseball fan. It's too slow. And it's too dangerous. Two words that seem incongruous side-by-side, but both true of baseball. I went out for baseball as a ten-year-old and lasted all of one practice. Some of the kids who played the year before had brought their own balls, bats and gloves and before the coaches arrived, began a little pick up practice of their own. Last year's pitcher and catcher lined up against last years best batter. I watched from the sidelines intently. Just how good were these guys?

It took one pitch to find out.

In came the fast ball, hot and slick—"Swoosh" went the bat as a mighty swing was taken—"Pip," went the wood of the bat as it grazed the spinning ball and . . . "AGGGGHHH-HHH!!!" went the catcher as the ball smacked him square in the eye. Within twenty seconds it was as big as an orange and blue as a violet. From what I hear the kid never came back that year. I say "from what I hear," because I didn't either.

The first words out of my mouth when picked up after practice were, "not my sport mom."

"But dear you didn't even . . . "

"I don't play baseball."

Whispering Loud and Clear

"But don't you think you should . . . "

"Ask the kid over there in the emergency room." I pointed to Roanoke Memorial Hospital located adjacent to the park.

"Emergency room?"

No further discussion required. Mom was now firmly in my camp, and the discussion with Dad went much the better for it. She, like I, was fine with basketball, soccer and even football, but heaving an eight ounce thinly covered rock at each other was no longer acceptable sport.

As an adult, I have absolutely no interest in baseball outside of the occasional minor league game that provides a wonderful venue in which to while away a summer evening. It's hard to beat the ambiance of hot dogs, peanuts, pretzels and cold beer while a game that is part ballet, part poker, part chess match, takes place on the well-groomed field below. Sitting there amongst the great cross-section of society, it's easy to understand how baseball became such a uniquely wonderful American tradition—the national pastime if you're not counting checkers and politics.

But how anyone could ever spend more than twelve seconds watching a televised broadcast, I'll never know. If you watch baseball on TV, you are either: A. So rich you have nothing else you need to do and your TV tuner is broken. Or B. So poor you can't afford to do anything else and your TV tuner is broken.

But I do enjoy watching our children play their little league games, and the other night we were treated to a great one. It was a "great one" because son George, got a hit. Getting a hit might not seem like such a big deal, but in the first year of "Player Pitch," where the eight to ten-year-olds are pitching themselves, connecting with the ball is cause for celebration. In fact, "not getting hit" by the ball itself is a bit of a victory.

Accuracy is being strived for, but it is hardly mastered.

The Best and Worst of Baseball

The teams generally score by players being walked to first base and then stealing the rest while the pitcher attempts to control his throws. The end result is a series of close plays being made between the catcher, who chases down the ball, and either the second or third baseman depending on where the runner happens to be. It makes for pretty good sport, but it's not exactly the pastime as Mickey Mantle or Joe Dimaggio knew it.

So the other night when George connected squarely with a rogue winner of a pitch, sending it into the green grass of the outfield, we were all ecstatic.

"HOLY COW," were the first words out of my mouth. . . "RUN GEORGE, RUN!!"

George took off as fast as his little legs would carry him and made it easily to first. His coaches yelled their approval . . . mom gushed a bit . . . his Grandparents beamed with pride . . .

Dad thought scholarship.

George managed to steal second and then third and then finally home, as the pitcher careened one off the top of the catcher's helmet. It was close, but a pretty decent slide added to the score. The Final—SW Cardinals: 12, Team of Unknown Origin: 2.

After the game, George was beaming. He received several extra high fives from his teammates as he left the field. He was moderately giddy but he had a certain calm about him, too. A few minutes later, with just he and I riding home alone together, I ask him how it felt to hit that ball.

"It was the greatest moment of my life," came the response. George is a rather level-headed eight year old and not one for great swings of emotion. It was about the last thing I expected to hear.

"The greatest moment of your life?" I queried. George paused several seconds. He finally responded.

"Dad . . . it wasn't like I hit that ball. I mean it was like

Whispering Loud and Clear

someone else did . . . it didn't seem like I was really paying attention . . . and then the next thing I know I can see the ball and the bat slowly coming to meet it, and then POP! There it went . . . It was really strange—but it felt really, really good . . . "

I smiled quietly in the front seat. I remembered the first time such a thing happened to me. At about his age, I was playing a friendly game of neighborhood softball with what were mostly older kids. I was standing dreamily out past first base somewhere short of where an outfielder might be when, "CRACK!" one of the older kids laid heavily into a buttercup pitch served up just for him. I was counting clouds or sorting clovers with my toes or some such thing, when the sound of bat to ball brought me out of my stupor just in time to watch myself make a diving catch of a line drive that would have made Ozzie Smith proud.

The other kids cheered wildly as I came up with the ball. All I could think was, "How in the world did that happen?"

Several years later, playing Sandlot football, I had an equally mysterious experience while going up to catch a pass that would enable us to get to the Championship game. Time had stood still as my body moved through the air not entirely under my own volition, and even before I hit the ground I knew that somehow, from somewhere in all the powers that rule the universe, I had just been given a very unique bit of assistance. My old football coach still talks about it every time I see him.

"Cheese and crackers, Revercomb—How you caught that football, I'll never know . . . "

But I think I do. And I told George as much.

"George, I'm not sure I can do a good job explaining it, but what you received tonight was a very special gift . . . a moment when, for reasons that you and I will probably never understand, everything lined up just right, and a window of sorts was opened somewhere . . . a window, that

188

The Best and Worst of Baseball

allowed time and space to flow through in some manner that we don't experience every day—or even ever for many of us. I myself, can think of only three or four such experiences, and I count them among the most precious of my life . . . so I know what you mean when you say it was the most wonderful experience of yours . . . " George sat quietly for several moments.

"Why do you think that happened Dad?" he finally asked.

"Well son, I don't know," I replied. "But I think it has something to do with desiring something just the right amount—not too much and not too little . . . a balance of sorts that finds us in the perfect moment at the perfect time with just the right perspective . . . when our bodies somehow become a conveyor of Grace that allows the physical part of our nature to become the expression of something more . . . " I glanced in the rearview mirror at George who was staring out over the darkening landscape.

"I think it has a lot to do with Trust" . . . I said.

"Maybe so . . . ," he replied. "I will never, ever forget it."

"Neither will I . . . ," I responded.

We stayed up late together and raided the fridge after his shower.

Baseball's not so bad.

40

The Greatest Stories Are the Untold Stories . . .

My old neighbors were two elderly sisters. Mae and Ida Reilly were in their 80's when my friend, Buzz, and I rented the apartment next door. Somewhat infirm of body they generally kept to themselves, and being true to form for elderly ladies the world over, they NEVER asked for help. Buzz and I used to wander over every couple of weeks to see if we could do anything.

"No sir, Stuart—everything's just fine . . . except the weather—can't do anything about the weather can you?" Mae always disarmed me by addressing me as sir. But Mae was not a formal person. "Isn't he the cutest thing," she'd continue, while smiling down at their Jack Russell Terrier that was viciously attacking my ankle. We never worried about the Reilly's security—that Jack Russell could fend off anything. He made his way through my socks and into my ankle bone on several occasions. I remember thinking it was probably a good thing they didn't call us over too often.

But every now and then, obstacles would come up that did require help. The first such request to come down the pipe was a light bulb change in a fixture that Mae couldn't reach with her ladder. Eighty-five year olds shouldn't even own ladders, but you couldn't convince Mae of that. Thankfully, she knew which step was one too many. Buzz headed over to perform the task, and didn't show back up for a couple of hours. When he finally did arrive, he had a smile on his face and a very, very old looking bottle of Scotch Whiskey in his hand.

"What took you so long?" I asked.

"Well, I changed the bulb in about two minutes," Buzz replied. "But then the Reilly sisters felt like they owed me some cookies and a story, so we all sat down and they told me several. One of them had to do with their father, who they mentioned was a connoisseur of very old Scotch. The next thing I know we're in the basement looking at his collection . . . one that apparently ended when he died in the 1940's . . . "

"You're not saying that . . . "

"Yup. It's all still down there. . . the girls don't touch the stuff." He handed me the bottle, and I beheld the old tan label with large block letters. "Black and White," it said. "Product of Scotland—By Appointment to Her Majesty The Queen." On the back were two Scottish Terriers, one white, one black. Beneath them were the words, "Distilled and Bottled in Scotland Under British Government Supervision." I guess the Brits didn't fancy the Scots reliable enough to produce Scotch in the Queen's name on their own. Being of Scottish Presbyterian descent, I was somewhat offended, but nevertheless intrigued at what might await inside.

"I don't know that anyone's ever been paid quite like you have for changing a light bulb," I said sarcastically.

"I tried to say no . . . several times," Buzz contended. I believed him. Knowing Mae and Ida, they were more than adamant he take it.

We uncorked the small bottle (You don't find many corks in Scotch bottles these days). Two quick sips confirmed our suspicions. He'd been given a treasure. Over the

The Greatest Stories Are the Untold Stories...

next three years we only partook of its contents on special occasions—small drams on Birthdays, New Years and Christmas Eve.

When it finally ran out, we put the bottle on the mantle above our fireplace. For a couple of young bachelors it was irreplaceable.

I think we had a ceremony. Buzz may have cried. I don't remember.

But the real treasure of visits with the Reillys didn't come from their basement or even their father's old cache. The real treasures were their stories. Little ones about "Mae's first date" and "Ida's adventures at nursing school," and especially the overarching story that was their lives. The Reilly sisters grew up in the 1920's and endured World War II while in their early 30's. Ida was a nurse fairly close to the front lines somewhere in Europe. Mae was a shipyard worker in Newport News.

Ida was quiet and sweet—overweight in the later part of her life as a result of two bad knees that she would have had replaced if the technology had been available. But as it was, she endured the pain and inconvenience of her disability with quiet persistence and grace. She gave her smile freely and was ever the optimist. She was one of the few people who could make her sister laugh.

Mae was thin and wiry and as feisty as her scrappy little dog, and looking at her determined face and worn skin, it was easy to imagine her as the quintessential "Rosie the Riveter." She showed me pictures of herself standing with several other ladies in front of one of the many "Liberty Ships" they helped to assemble along the steaming docks of Hampton Roads. Mae was vibrant and healthy looking in the photo, with a bandanna around her hair and a broad smile on her face. It was a distant likeness, but the connection could be made easily enough to the face that glowed so brightly when she brought out those old pictures.

Whispering Loud and Clear

The stories they told were of good times pulling together with family and friends and of bad times pulling together with family and friends—of simple events and moments that changed a life here or there, and / or taught them what it was all about. Listening to them reflect on their lives, taught me no small amount of wisdom either:

- The best things in life are simple and plain and not likely the things you dreamed of as a teenager.

- The most meaningful moments come almost entirely unexpected and in ways that no Hollywood screenwriter could ever conceive.

- God has his plan—even if he isn't always willing or able to share it. Trust him.

The very best stories? The largely untold stories like Mae and Ida's—the ones you and I will likely never hear . . . of men and women who give of themselves through small acts of kindness and support to those who cross their paths. Folks who know what being a human being in the best sense is all about. Such individuals might not get a chapter written about them in the "World Book" or next year's edition of "Encarta," but they do provide the very best verses in the ongoing books of Hope and Faith and Love that make up the whole of God's great library.

In the end, they're the only ones that matter.

*THIS
BUILDING Was
Erected In The year
1796 At The Expense
Of A Few Of The First
Inhabitants of This
Land To Commemorate
Their Affection &
Esteem For The
Holy Gospel of
JESUS CHRIST*

*Reader
If You Are Inclined
To Applaud Their
Virtues Give GOD
The Glory*

- Chiseled into the rock by the builders of
"The Old Stone Presbyterian Church,"
Lewisburg, West Virginia.